From

The Women's Press Ltd
34 Great Sutton Street, London EC1V 0DX

Barbara Wilson

Barbara Wilson was born in Long Beach, California, in 1950. She is a co-founder of Seal Press, Seattle, where she works as an editor. Her previous books include *Murder in the Collective* (The Women's Press, 1984), *Ambitious Women* (The Women's Press, 1983), and two collections of stories, *Thin Ice* and *Walking on the Moon* (The Women's Press, 1986). Her translation of *Cora Sandel: Selected Short Stories* won a Columbia Translation Center Award, and she has also translated *Nothing Happened*, a novel by Ebba Haslund.

Barbara Wilson
Sisters of the Road

The Women's Press

First published in Great Britain by The Women's Press Limited 1987
A member of the Namara Group
34 Great Sutton Street, London EC1V 0DX

British Library Cataloguing in Publication Data

Wilson, Barbara, *1950*
Sisters of the road.
I. Title
813'.54[F]   PS3573.I45678
ISBN 0-7043-5028-9
ISBN 0-7043-4073-9 Pbk

Printed and bound by Hazell Watson & Viney Ltd, Aylesbury, Bucks.

Acknowledgments

Many people helped me in the research and writing of this novel. In particular I'd like to thank Guila Muir for hanging out with me on the streets of Seattle; Verna Wells, intrepid skydiver; Hylah Jacques for a night on the Sea-Tac Strip and valuable editorial comments; Debra Boyer for her information and insight; Evelyn C. White for much useful criticism; and Rachel da Silva, who notices the small things. Judith Barrington and Ruth Gundle provided a home away from home in Portland and many important contacts; Ruth in particular gave me all the legal advice I wanted – and more. Many social workers, activists and prostitutes gave generously of their time and experience. I was also very much helped by Liv Finstad and Cecilie Høigaard in Norway and by their groundbreaking research on juvenile prostitution in their book *Bakgater (Back Streets)*. I would especially like to thank Jen Green of The Women's Press in London and Faith Conlon at Seal Press for editorial support and advice that made all the difference.

Acknowledgements

For Faith

1

"Good-bye," I whispered. Outside the airport's plate glass windows the lights of the jet floated eerily upwards and disappeared into the night and thick cloudcover; snowflakes fell like confetti at a ghostly leave-taking. Seattle to Mexico City, Mexico City to Managua. My twin sister Penny and her boyfriend Ray were off to help with Nicaragua's coffee bean harvest for six weeks.

Bon voyage, buen viaje. Love and resentment, the two emotions I most often associated with my sister, flared up suddenly, destroying the jovial, all-for-the-revolution mood I'd so carefully cultivated and acted out at Gate Six, Mexicana Airlines. Except for a misguided effort on our parents' part one summer to send us to different relatives, Penny and I had never been parted by such a great distance before.

Our friends began to move away, hurrying to get home before the weather got worse.

"It's going to be a long six weeks for you and the print shop without them, isn't it?" Penny's friend Miranda said sympathetically.

June and I looked at each other. Our collective had argued for

3

six months over whether we could manage without Penny and Ray, and still there was no way we could predict what it would be like. And no way we could stop them from going. If the U.S. ever did invade Nicaragua we'd be sorry we hadn't done our bit.

"January's a slow month," said June, hugging herself tighter into her heavy wool jacket. Underneath her red beret her small cocoa-brown features showed a sad resignation. She and Penny had gotten very close over the fall, pursuing their favorite sport – sky-diving. They'd even formed a women's skydiving club and pooled their money with friends to hire airplanes to drop them out of the air every other weekend. Someone like me, who couldn't even manage to get up on the low diving board without feeling my stomach sink to my toes, would not be a good substitute.

I linked my arm in June's and spoke cheerfully. "We've got Carole doing the camera work now. And there's a guy who'll help with layout and stripping if we need him. He won't be part of the collective though, I mean, he won't have any decision-making power."

"Mmmm, great," said Miranda vaguely, anchoring her frizzy red hair more firmly inside the elastic band at the back of her head. She was a staff nurse at Harborview and the complexities of both printing and printing collectives were lost on her. Nothing could be more hierarchical than a hospital. She looked at her watch. "I'd better hurry if I'm going to get to work by eleven. I hate the thought of driving in this stuff though." She gestured out the window at the falling snow. "It's really dismal. Not like Central America, huh?"

June and I looked at each other again and laughed gloomily. Not a bit like Central America, we agreed.

I got into my Volvo in the airport garage and let it warm up. For six years it had been a trusted friend – now, like seemingly everything else in my life, it was kicking up. Burning oil and burping wounded little noises whenever I went over forty. The Volvo hadn't wanted to come to the airport tonight at all, and now it was rebelling against going home. It wanted gas too; I'd better stop at a station outside the airport. I wished June had driven with me, and not only because she was so good in auto-motive emergencies. I could have used the company.

4

All the gas stations were off the freeway on Pacific Highway South, also known as the Sea-Tac Strip — a long necklace with a jewelled cluster of Hyatts and Hiltons at the center and tawdry pearls and rhinestones of cheap motels, taverns, go-go dancer bars and Burger Kings strung out a mile in either direction. The street that was so often mentioned as the "last place seen." The last place a girl or young woman had been seen before she turned up as a heap of bones and teeth to be identified in some wooded, desolate spot nearby.

They called them the Green River murders because the first remains had been discovered by the Green River. In the months and years since then, boy scouts, hikers and picnickers had found almost three dozen corpses or skulls and bones all over the area south of Seattle, and more women were missing. Some estimates ranged in the seventies. The investigation had bogged down over and over, but whenever a new set of remains was found the newspapers regurgitated the whole story and sometimes printed a list of the murdered. Wendy Lee Coffield, Debra Lynn Bonner, Opal Charmaine Mills. They all had three names, with a number from fifteen to twenty-five after them. Their ages. They were runaways and prostitutes, the papers said, and went on with touching articles about their foster parents or their single mothers, who all said they didn't know where the girl had gone wrong. None of the dead were women that I or any of my friends knew. We didn't know any prostitutes.

At the station I filled the tank, put in oil and looked into the engine — not that I could have figured out what was wrong. I decided that if the Volvo lasted until spring I'd sell it. Maybe I should even sell it now, while it was still running.

Back inside the car I drove up what looked like a main street and went a couple of blocks before I realized I was going in the wrong direction to get back to the freeway. There was nothing up here but cheap motels advertising adult channels and waterbeds; most of them were too shoddy even to be lurid and they all had vacancies. The snow was falling faster now and it was difficult to see. I pulled into an apartment complex to turn around. It was a badly illuminated, sinister set of buildings with a peeling sign that said Bella Vista: Deluxe Suites Available.

Reversing, the car stalled and died. The wet snow began to pile up on the windshield, on the passenger side where the wiper didn't work as well.

Don't panic, I told myself sternly. Just two blocks away, the benevolent yellow neon of a Denny's restaurant gleamed at me. Where there's a Denny's, there's twenty-four hour safety. I'd give the Volvo a couple of tries and then call June if it wouldn't start. She'd be home in ten minutes.

But, grumbling, the car came to life again and I began to back up. Out of a gap to my right, behind me, between two of the dimly lit apartment buildings, stepped two figures, one supporting the other and both of them weaving drunkenly. They seemed to be making towards me, and I kept reversing as far to the left as I could. As I went past, the taller one, the one who was supporting the other, gestured to me to stop. I had an impression—but no, they were both wearing hats—it was too dark and thick with snow to see clearly—but even if they were women—to pick up two drunks—in this part of town...I kept staring at them as the car reached the sidewalk. The one had slumped over and the other was trying to drag her. Yes, they were women, they looked quite young, they looked like teenagers.

I put on the brakes and skidded slightly, then began to accelerate cautiously forward again. When I got alongside of them I could see that one was Black and one was white and they were only about sixteen or seventeen, wearing hats and thin leather jackets and tight jeans and, of all incredible things on this night, high-heeled shoes with thin straps.

I leaned over and rolled down the passenger window, shouting, "Hurry up before you freeze to death. There's a blanket in the back. Get in and tell me where you want to go."

The Black girl fell into the back seat and immediately passed out. The taller white girl, her face pinched and ghastly under heavy makeup, said breathlessly, "We want to go to downtown Seattle, to a place we're staying on Second Ave."

I nodded, still not sure if I should have picked them up—what if they mugged me?—and said, "What's the fastest way to the freeway entrance? Can you point it out?"

"Go back to the airport and get on that way. Could you hurry, please?" she asked in a strained and urgent voice. "We really want to get back. Rosalie isn't feeling too well."

Great. She was going to puke in my car; that should certainly add to its saleability. My voice sounded sharp and prim as I answered, "I'll drive as fast as it's safe to."

She didn't say anything. She wrapped the blanket closely around her sagging companion and stroked her shoulder.

"My name's Pam. What's yours?"

"Trish," she said reluctantly. In the rearview mirror she looked younger than I'd first imagined. The black felt hat was pulled down over a triangular face with widely-set, black-ringed eyes and two patches of blusher like red gauze pasted on her cheeks. Strands of wet hair streamed below the hat, and earrings made of many thin chains hung down past her pointed chin.

I found the freeway at last and entered slowly. The traffic was moving erratically, divided equally between drivers who were determined to pretend that nothing out of the ordinary was happening, that this really wasn't a snow storm and that they could still drive as fast as they wanted, and those like me, weather cowards, who were practically holding their cars by the hand and walking them.

I turned up the heater, which was fortunately working tonight, and fiddled with the radio, which wasn't. Static and irritating gusts of country-western music. No news or weather reports. I probably didn't want to hear about the hazardous driving conditions anyway.

"Please," came a small, insistent voice from the back seat. "Can't you go any faster?"

"No," I said shortly. "I don't know what your hurry is. Your friend can sleep it off just as well here in the car as anywhere else."

"She's not sleeping," Trish said, and now I caught her panic. "I can't wake her up. She was, somebody, I mean, she's hurt . . ."

I turned around with a jerk just as Trish raised Rosalie's head for me to see. Blood was running from somewhere under her hat, running down her neck and inside her jacket. There was a thin trickle coming from her mouth too, and her eyes rolled under half-closed lids.

"Shit!" I said, then gripped the wheel firmly and stepped on the gas.

7

2

AMBULANCES WERE PULLING up to Harborview's emergency room like chauffeured cars at the opera, one every few minutes —the only difference being that their occupants came out on stretchers, wrapped in blankets instead of furs, with portable I.V.'s decorating their arms instead of diamond bracelets.

I left the car in the driveway and ran inside. It was Sunday night; the waiting room was packed and the reception desk six deep in supplicants. Short of screaming there was no way to get any of the staff's attention. But when an orderly walked by, I lunged for his arm. "Please get a stretcher, there's a girl who's badly hurt—hit on the head."

He was grabbing a stretcher and pushing it towards the door even as I tried to explain that I didn't know anything about her or how it had happened.

"Where?" he snapped, cutting me off.

I ran to my car and opened the back door. Rosalie's head was in Trish's lap; she looked as if she weren't breathing.

The orderly took her pulse. "Barely," he said. "Help me lift."

Trish shrank back into a corner of the seat. There was blood

8

on her hands and jeans, and her face was as white as her leather jacket.

Rosalie was on the stretcher. "Follow me," said the orderly, "And tell them about it at the desk. They'll call the police."

I nodded, numb, and watched him disappear through the door with Rosalie. "Come on," I said to Trish. "Come with me and tell them how it happened."

"I'm not talking to the police," she said, squeezing herself fearfully away from me.

"You listen to me." I blew up suddenly. "Your girlfriend's seriously hurt . . . for godssakes, why didn't you tell me right away something had happened to her, instead of waiting until we were halfway to Seattle?"

She said nothing and refused to look at me, but blackish tears ran down her face. I got into the back seat. "I don't mean to yell at you, Trish, but it's important. Were you with her when it happened? Was it a . . . customer of hers? If you could give them a description, anything, a car license number — they could look for him . . ."

"You the lady who brought the girl in?" asked another orderly outside the car. "Can you come to the desk and answer some questions?"

"You stay right here," I told Trish. "I'll be back in a minute and we'll talk some more."

I went back into the emergency room and gave my name and address. I told them where I'd picked up the two girls and that I hadn't known Rosalie was hurt until at least fifteen minutes later.

"Just off Pacific Highway South," repeated the nurse and looked at me. She knew about the Green River murders too. "The police should be here shortly. And what about the other girl? Is she all right? She wasn't hurt at all?"

I realized I didn't know. "She seems kind of stunned," I said. "She doesn't want to come in, or talk about it."

"We can give her something," said the nurse. "What's her name?"

"Trish."

"Age?"

"Seventeen?"

The nurse looked depressed. "I hate to see it."

The orderly who'd first brought Rosalie in came through the

9

swinging doors that led to the procedure room. I went over. "How is she?"

"Not good," he said, with a blank kindness that showed he'd been running on high for too long. "She hasn't come to and she's lost a lot of blood." He went to the desk and said something in a low voice to the nurse. Then a new ambulance roared up with lights flashing and sirens wailing, and he was out the door.

For the first time I looked around the waiting room. It seemed full of elderly and homeless people seeking medical attention, or just trying to get out of the cold. They sat in their worn, ragged coats and tired shoes, with plastic bags and stuffed pillow cases at their feet. More anxious, more restless were the friends and relatives of victims, who paced back and forth, looked at their watches, said the same reassuring things over and over to each other and kept going up to the desk to ask if there was any news yet.

"Are you Miss Nilsen?" A uniformed cop and a plainclothes detective had come up behind me. "Mind if we ask you some questions?"

There was nowhere to sit so we stood in a corner. Such was the fear, worry and depression in the room that hardly anyone bothered to pay attention to us.

I told them what I'd told the nurse—that I'd taken my sister to the airport, stopped to get some gas and had made a wrong turn. It was a couple blocks off the strip. The Bella Vista. I didn't know what room the girls had come out of.

"Any other cars around? Any people?" They pressed me quietly and thoroughly.

I asked, "Do you think this may have some connection to the Green River murders?"

The cop shrugged. "You never know. It may have just been some guy who was mad at getting ripped off by two teenage hookers. They were working together, it looks like."

"You're suggesting that maybe she deserved it?"

The more politic detective said somewhat wearily, "No, of course not." It was clear he'd pegged me as some kind of commie feminist and didn't want to argue. "Can we see the other girl now? She's still in your car?"

"Yes." But I felt protective of Trish suddenly. What if they wanted to take her down to the station? What would happen to

10

her there? She'd been so upset – she needed kindness and sympathy – not an insensitive, offensive grilling. I'd just have to stay with her somehow.

Through the darkness and falling snow I pointed out the Volvo. The headlights were still on, but it looked empty. "She must be lying down," I said, flinging open the back door. There was plenty of blood, but no Trish. And my bag, with my wallet and everything?

"Looks like she's skipped," said the cop.

"Lose anything?" asked the detective, watching my face.

Damned if they were going to get the satisfaction of knowing that Trish had ripped me off. "No." I turned off the lights and noticed with relief that at least the keys were still in the ignition. I took them out. What a fool I'd been. Driver's license, checkbook, Sears credit card, and two tickets to the Laurie Anderson concert . . . at least I still had my glasses; they were on my nose. Most depressing was the loss of the day's bank deposit for Best Printing. In the frenzy of helping Penny get ready to leave I hadn't managed to get to the bank in time. It wasn't a lot of money, but we still couldn't afford to lose it. I'd have to make the cash up myself and put stops on the checks tomorrow. June wasn't going to be too pleased.

"We may be getting in touch with you again," said the detective, and read me my address and phone to make sure he'd gotten it right. "And if you run into that girl again – see if you can get her name. Or give me a call and tell me where you've seen her."

"Or if you want to report anything stolen," said the cop.

I went back into the hospital, shivering. The waiting room was even more crowded than before, and had a wet, rank smell to it. I asked for news of Rosalie and got nothing, so I went to the pay phone and called Miranda's floor upstairs. She came down right away, sympathetic, but with that same supercharged, overworked but holding-it-all-together efficiency I'd noticed in everyone on the staff.

I told her what was going on.

"All this has happened since I saw you at the airport two hours ago?" For a moment she was the incredulous girl Penny and I used to tease on the grade school playground, then she became

11

Miranda the nurse again, impervious to bad news. "I'll see what I can find out."

She went to the desk and exchanged a few words with the nurse, then slipped through the big swinging doors. In five minutes she was back.

"She was hit on the back of the head with a heavy blunt instrument, a crowbar or tire iron, something like that. Her skull is fractured and there's severe trauma to both hemispheres of the brain. I'm afraid that if she does survive..." Miranda didn't finish, and I filled in the words to myself: paralyzed, a vegetable.

Miranda put an arm around me. "I'm so sorry, Pam—but you should know that even if you'd called an ambulance right away, it probably wouldn't have made any difference. Does she have any family?"

"No one knows what her last name is. She didn't have an ID."

"What monster could have done something like that?" She shivered. "I've got to get back to my floor, it's busy up there. If you want to stay, give me another call in an hour and I'll come down."

"Thanks, Miranda."

I paced at first, then found an empty seat next to an old woman who was mumbling something about canaries taking over the world, and who stank of urine and unwashed clothes. It wasn't so much that I thought Trish would come back—though I certainly didn't quite stop hoping she might, as much for my wallet and the deposit as for wanting to know she cared about Rosalie—but that I obscurely and tenaciously felt Rosalie needed someone there, sending her strength, mourning the loss of her future. If it couldn't be her mother or father, sisters or brothers, it would have to be me, a stranger she hadn't even been able to talk to.

I waited forty-five minutes and was just about to call Miranda when the brisk orderly came through the swinging doors and looked around. I sensed somehow he was looking for me and I went over to him.

"I'm sorry to tell you," he said, and then paused uncharacteristically. Pain surfaced in his eyes and then was controlled again. "The girl you brought in. She's dead."

12

3

By THE TIME I GOT HOME it was past two in the morning. No one was up to greet me, just as there had been no one to call and tell I'd be late. At the late age of thirty, I was living alone for the first time.

Last summer I'd moved out of the home I'd shared for years with Penny and our two housemates. At first it had been exciting to set up house by myself. The apartment I'd found was a spacious one in an old ivy-covered brick building on Capitol Hill. It was on the fourth floor and the living room window had a lavish western view of Queen Anne Hill and Elliott Bay. I'd watched sunset after sunset all through the summer and fall, and life had seemed, if not perfect, then more than tolerable. The space and the sunsets went together with a sense of independence less tinged with melancholy than I'd dreaded. I'd bought plants and put up posters and learned to cook for one from the section in the *Enchanted Broccoli Forest* called "Light Meals for Nibblers."

But by the end of fall my solitude no longer seemed quite so adventurous. Starting in November I found myself going through an unusually promiscuous phase. My affair with Hadley last summer had removed me from my old circle of heterosexual friends, and I threw myself into a string of one-night and one-week stands with women, out of curiosity and need, and as if to confirm all my worried sister's worst fears about lesbians and their rampantly unstable sex lives.

Over a period of two months I slept with four women—well, maybe that wasn't so promiscuous; for plenty of people that was a way of life. For Carole at the shop for instance, who went through relationships like new breakfast cereals. But for me, with my vague ideas about commitment, who'd had maybe four boyfriends and Hadley my whole life, it felt pretty daring. I didn't regret it—I'd learned a lot—but I was thinking about taking a breather. For one thing, it was all so complicated: not starting up, no that was easy, but maintaining an interest, and even worse, breaking off.

Not that most of the women weren't very nice people—Betty was a classical guitarist and played me a little Bach chaconnes and gaviots while I ate my breakfast; Andrea made me whole-wheat pastries and breads until I felt like a grain terminal (batches of muffins still kept turning up forlornly on my doorstep); Dandi gave wonderful massages and Devlin told great stories. But somehow none of them were quite the ticket. After a shorter or longer period I'd find myself yawning and struggling to keep a conversation going, avoiding places where I might meet one of them, and looking around eagerly for someone new, someone who might be *the one*. I was afraid of admitting to myself what I knew was true—my time with Hadley, short as it had been, had spoiled me. Not only was that the sort of relationship I wanted, but that's *who* I still wanted.

I never talked about her to anyone, didn't know how to talk about her. I didn't have the words to describe what I'd felt with her. The nearest I could come was the phrase, "We were so regular together." Sometimes I wondered if it had ever really happened. I would have liked to ask her, but she wasn't even in Seattle any longer. Her father had had a stroke and she'd gone back to Houston to help take care of him. A postcard with a skyscraper skyline had arrived one day in December and its message had been as uninspiring as its view: "I miss Seattle, but not the rain. My accent's coming back with a vengeance. You'd probably laugh to hear me."

Nothing about giving me the opportunity.

I went around my apartment, nervously turning on lights, trying not to think too much about what had happened at the hospital. But the image of blood running down Rosalie's face, of Trish's black-rimmed, frightened eyes wouldn't leave me. They were so young to be on their own, so young to be using their sexuality, and used for it.

Rosalie was dead now, and Trish was running. From who, from what? From me, because I'd pushed her? I should have handled it differently, should have handled the whole thing differently. But I'd been afraid of them, hadn't really looked at them. Just hadn't seen them.

In the kitchen I opened the refrigerator out of habit rather than hunger. In a flash Ernesto was there, roused from whatever deep feline sleep he'd been enjoying by the prospect of food. Ernesto was Ray's cat and I had promised to take care of him while Ray was away. It had been a weak moment and I was regretting it.

Ernesto was as profusely furred as a mohair sweater and as solid as a tank; big as a dog, but without a dog's friendly, trusting eyes. Ernesto's gaze was superior, distant and calculating. Even during the time Ray and I had been involved I hadn't liked Ernesto much. He had a way of ignoring me when I tried to get his attention that made me feel foolish—and a way of being physically aggressive just when I was least interested, when I was trying to sleep, for instance. Now I faced six weeks of his company, a fact that didn't seem to excite him either. For when it became obvious that he wasn't going to be fed, he contemplated me severely and gloomily for a moment before turning and padding heavily back to whatever dark recess of the apartment he'd emerged from.

Next to food, sleep was most interesting to Ernesto—and after a few more minutes of bleakly staring at the contents of my refrigerator—old tofu, an open can of tomato paste, six bottles of salad dressing and three withered carrots—I decided he was right and went to bed.

4

WHEN I WOKE UP five hours later the world had that remarkable stillness that comes after a storm, when everything is embedded in a white as soft as cotton. The sky was opalescent with a few rosy clouds and the city had a unified look only a snow cover can give. There was almost no traffic; from the fourth floor I couldn't even hear the scrunch of boots or the scrape of shovels, just here and there the rumble of an engine trying to start. For a moment, before I remembered last night's events, I felt only peace and a childish wish to stay home from school and take my sled over to the park.

Then I started rooting around in the closet for long underwear, heavy socks and boots. I found my old yellow-striped knit cap with the white pompom and the blue scarf and mitten set my mother had given me the Christmas before the car accident that had killed her and my father. Penny had gotten a red version; every year our mother gave us some little thing that matched. At the age of five we'd liked our gifts, at ten refused them, at fifteen returned them to the store, and at twenty finally accepted them. Now the blue scarf and mittens reminded me of both my mother

16

and Penny and I was glad to wear them.

I didn't drive my car—I'd be glad never to get into it again after last night. Now it had blood—Rosalie's blood, smear-dried all over the back seat. No wonder Trish hadn't wanted to stay in the Volvo. But my bag! And the deposit!

The Monday morning scene up on Broadway was less than peaceful. The street had been plowed and sprinkled with sand, and shivering crowds stood waiting for the slow trolleys. We weren't too used to snow in Seattle. Those who skied were well-turned out in bright jackets and caps; everyone else looked like they'd thrown on whatever they could find to keep them warm. Still, the spirit was lively and strangers traded excited complaints and stories: "I could barely get out my door this morning." "*My* street is one of those that *never* gets plowed—and then it just turns to *ice*." "Did your pipes freeze too?" "Remember the winter of '79? This is really nothing compared to that. I bet this is gone by tomorrow." "Well, the kids love it anyway."

We packed ourselves into the trolley like frozen string beans and began to expand and cook in the heat. The trolley lurched down the hill and through the city center. "It's going to be a hard day," department store clerks complained. "Those girls in Bothell will say they were snowed in." But others looked forward to an easier rhythm. Things would go on as usual, just more slowly.

June was at the print shop before me and said that Carole had called to say she'd just gotten back into town after a weekend away and had found her pipes frozen. She'd be in late.

"You could have expected it," said June, and I agreed. In her very unreliability, Carole was predictable. Giddy, endearing and exasperating, Carole bounced from one complication to the next, chronically late and astonishingly absent-minded. Every day she lost the keys to her car; every day the thing she most needed disappeared in some mysterious way.

She'd been working with Best Printing for six months, and kept us all in a state of confusion, as we tried to help her find things and occasionally burst out in frustration, "Carole, what are you *doing*?"

In spite of thinking she was completely hopeless, I had been attracted to her on more than one occasion. I'd never let her know. Life was complicated enough already.

"You didn't drive, did you?" asked June. "I thought about it, but the streets are a mess."

I thought about the Volvo's back seat again and the whole story came pouring out. It sounded unreal and bizarre on this cold white morning. "And then I waited and waited and then they said Rosalie was dead."

"Rosalie, Rosalie. I used to know a Rosalie. I mean, she was a kid who went to our church. Skinny and braids? Probably not any more. I should call my cousin, my cousin knows everybody. What about that other girl, what was her name—Trish? What the fuck was her trip, taking off like that?"

The muscles in June's cocoa face tightened, like machinery parts that have gone too fast and seized up, and her brown eyes blazed. "Stupid little bitches, seventeen years old and they think they know everything and can protect themselves. They've undercut the whole prostitution racket and they don't think they can learn anything from women who've been working the street for years. You see many women over twenty-five getting knocked off by the Green River killer? No, because they know how to protect themselves."

June had jumped up and taken hold of a chair as if ready to bring it down over someone's head. I didn't dare bring up the problem of the missing deposit right now. "And you think that goddamn Green River Task Force is out there telling the girls to be careful, telling them what they know about this guy, his little perversions and all? Thirty girls' bodies found and maybe there's fifty more. Yeah, if they were from Bellevue or Broadmoor or someplace you can bet they'd have found the guy and sent him up for life plus two thousand years. Little Rosalie No-Name. Poor little Black Rosalie No-Name! I'm going to call my cousin right now."

I went to the window and stared out. There were about two inches of snow; probably it wouldn't stay long. One elderly guy in a long taupe coat was picking his way slowly down the street. I remembered the packed waiting room at Harborview; the homeless were everywhere these days.

"Yeah, ask her to call me back," June was saying. Her anger had vanished and she just sounded efficient. She and Penny were two of a kind, organized, model hard workers. "Gotta start running that poster job," she said, out of her chair before she hung up the receiver.

But the phone rang again. "It's for you," June said, and in a stage whisper, "One of your old girlfriends."

Old was a misnomer for this one, Devlin, who still considered herself very much in the running.

"Hello, Pam! Isn't the snow fantastic! I thought maybe you'd like to come on up to my house after work and we could take a walk and then have dinner and I could make a fire."

I remembered those little fireside chats that had quickly grown so personal. Devlin had had an interesting life of travel and adventure; unfortunately she was definitely into recounting it at length. After episode four (Nepal, the summer of '74), I'd had enough.

"I don't think so, Devlin." I wasn't unsympathetic to people nursing hopeless crushes; my own undying feelings for Hadley fell into pretty much the same category, but at least I had the dignity to shut up about it. "I'm fairly busy today...I...I have to wash my car."

There was a silence as frosty as the air outside. "Well, I must say you've chosen an excellent day for it," she snarled and hung up.

"You're so popular, Pam," June said.

"Yeah, now I have four new enemies that I didn't have before."

"Well, everybody has to sow their wild oats sometime."

"I feel a little old for this though."

"It's only because you came out so late," she said wisely, as if she were my ancient dyke great-aunt and not a practicing heterosexual five years younger. "You have to make up for lost time. You'll settle down some day."

The phone rang again and this time it was her cousin Joyce. She knew everyone in the world, but she didn't think she knew a Rosalie. She'd tell the parents of the missing girls, though — maybe Rosalie was a fake name. Because Darla's Beverly was gone and so was Cheryl Brown, you know, that cute girl who used to sing so good in choir. She kind of hoped it wasn't her, hoped it was nobody they knew....

June got worked up again and said that the so-called Green River Task Force was probably getting paid by the killer to set the girls up. Probably the killer was even on the fucking task force! Somebody's idea of cleaning up the streets!

I looked out the frosted window again and saw another figure

19

picking its way through the snow. It too wore a beige coat, but this one was fashionable and swung open, unbuttoned, and I had seen that hat before. The figure was also carrying something very familiar. It stopped and looked at the building numbers, and by the time it reached our shop I had the door open. I was surprised at how relieved I was to see her.

"Come in, come in," I said. "June, this is Trish."

5

T HE YOUNG WOMAN who came through the door looked far different than she had last night in my car. That small, pathetic girl with the pale, terrified face under the black hat was actually taller than me, and the stiletto heels of her short soft leather boots made her even taller. Under her fake fur-lined coat she was wearing jeans and a red sweatshirt with a dash of black calligraphy across the front. Her figure was good, in a kind of unnatural Barbie Doll way: broad shoulders, spindly arms, large breasts, narrow hips and legs with almost no thigh. Today she was wearing no jewelry other than a silver heart on a chain around her neck, and very little makeup. Under her hat her small features were sharp and pointed; only the widely spaced eyes were outlined; the tiny rosebud mouth was pale and chapped. Strands of frosted ash-blond hair curled over her shoulders.

June and I were in overalls and hiking boots, and I still wore my tattered blue scarf around my neck.

"Have a seat," I said, and gestured to the couch. June said good-bye to her cousin, pulled up a chair and straddled it. I perched on the couch's armrest.

21

"I didn't take any checks or money or anything," Trish began, holding out my bag. Her voice was high and a little nasal; she consciously lowered it and started again. "I just wanted your address."

June looked severely at me and then at the bag, a dirty white canvas pouch with a leather strap. "Was the deposit in there? Give me that."

While I might have felt constrained from counting the money, June certainly didn't. She plunged her hand in and took out the deposit envelope, then tossed the bag over to me.

I said, "You know that Rosalie is . . . ."

"I know. I called the hospital."

"Was Rosalie her real name?" asked June. "What was her last name? Her parents ought to know."

"I don't think she has parents," said Trish. "She came from California. I didn't know her long, but . . ." she ducked her frosted head and opened up her purse, expensive soft leather like her boots. "She was my best friend."

I thought for a second she was crying, but when she raised her head again her eyes were dry and their expression distant. She took out a Marlboro and lit it with a cheap lighter. Her hands were small and skinny, child's hands, with artificial purplish fingernails attached to them like mussel shells.

She smoked badly, as if she had learned the art for an amateur play.

"I want to do something," she said. "But I don't want to talk to the police."

"Why not?" asked June.

"They'd tell my parents where I am. I don't want them to know. They live in Broadmoor—they'd just put me back in that awful girls' school I ran away from. In six months I'll be eighteen. I don't want them to know where I am until then."

"You hooking?" June asked.

"Not really."

"What do you mean, not really?"

"I have a friend," said Trish. She attempted to smile, and choked a little on her cigarette smoke.

"Then what were you doing down around Sea-Tac?" June shot back.

Trish didn't answer; she took a long, uncomfortable drag from her cigarette and looked at me.

"How can we help you?" I asked.

Her sudden look of panic went straight through me.

"I'm afraid," she whispered.

"Afraid? Afraid of what?"

"I don't know," she said. Her cigarette was burning close to her purple fingernails but she didn't seem to notice. "It was so dark and snowy. It took me a long time to get there and I was late – I feel like it's all my fault."

"Did you see the man? Would you recognize him again?" I leaned towards her from my perch on the armrest. "Is that who you're afraid of?"

"No," she said, with a thin, quavering vehemence, and stubbed out her cigarette on the floor. "I didn't see him. But I have this feeling – it makes me so afraid – that he saw me."

June and I conferred in the press room while Trish continued to smoke cigarettes out front. June had pointedly provided her with a saucer and told her to pick up the butt from the floor.

"Don't get involved in this, Pam. It's too weird. And you'll get dragged into it, I know how you are, and you won't pay attention to your work, and then it will be you *and* Carole flaking off."

"Just because Penny's gone you don't need to start acting like her. Christ, she was born two minutes before me and my whole life she's acted like my older sister. If you want to know something, her leaving was a relief and I don't need you telling me what to do."

"You think this girl is telling the truth? She is *not*. All that stuff about her parents and that guy supporting her? She's just a regular street hooker like the rest of them downtown. Before she goes you better take a good look in your wallet and see if all your credit cards are still there."

"She's not going to get far on a Sears card already charged up to its limit. Besides, I think Nordstrom's is more her style."

"Those clothes are all ripped off. Ripped off, I'm telling you. The girl is a con artist if I've ever seen one. Broadmoor, fancy girls' school, that's a load of shit. She's got something in mind you don't know the slightest bit about. I know these types of girls. I knew them in high school, hey, some are even my relatives."

23

There was nothing I could say to that. June had street smarts and I did not. But I trusted my instincts about Trish somehow. And I wasn't going to send her away without finding out more about her.

June finally accepted it. She turned to the press and started to load the paper and said, "I'm only promising you one thing—that I won't say I told you so when you get disappointed."

"Promise me one other thing."

"What's that?"

"That you won't say 'I told Pam so,' to Penny when she gets back."

And with a pitying smile June promised me that too.

6

I took Trish for an early lunch at the cafe downstairs from the Elliott Bay Book Company. The sun had appeared like a pale granite stone in the white-gray sky, and Occidental Square looked its old-fashioned, slightly touristy self; bare trees and grill-work, surrounded by solid masonry. Trish walked carefully in her high-heeled boots by my side and was noticed by passersby in ways I'd long forgotten. In my parka and overalls, yellow-striped cap pulled down over my ears, I felt like a woodsman escorting a fairy princess who had gone astray in the forest outside the castle.

The bookstore was crowded and so was the cafe. "This is like a library down here," Trish whispered. The cafe was lined with books, not for sale but for show — tired old bestsellers like *Forever Amber* and *Marjorie Morningstar* and old reference works and encyclopedias: "A–Pocket Veto"; "Pockmark–Zymurgy." I had always wondered what zymurgy meant.

"Do you like to read?" I asked her as we got into line.

"Oh, I love to!" Her sharp features lit up with genuine pleasure. "I love to read books that are really long and have good stories that keep you guessing. Did you ever read *Shōgun*?"

I shook my head.

"That was a really great book! It was, like, in Japan, only early Japan. You really learned a lot from it. Like history, but it was fun."

"Do you read many women authors?"

"Women authors? You mean, books by women?" She thought a minute. "Oh yeah! I read *Mistral's Daughter.* That was really great too. It was about three women, from different generations, and the first two were in love with this man and the third was his daughter. He was a great Parisian artist." She pronounced it Pareeshun very carefully. "They made a TV movie out of it. Didn't you see it?"

"I don't watch much TV." I wasn't going to tell her, or anyone else for that matter, that this winter I'd been tuning into the late movie and the late late movie and had even found myself crying over *The King and I.*

"Oh," said Trish. She turned her attention to the food and appeared slightly alarmed at the choices: mulligatawny soup, spanakopita, plates of Greek salads and Italian antipasto. "I'll take a roast beef sandwich on white bread," she told the woman behind the counter. "But don't put any lettuce or sprouts on it." She added a slice of mocha-almond torte and a Diet Pepsi to her tray. "Oh no, I just realized I left my wallet at home," she said nervously, looking into her bag. "How stupid!"

"My treat," I assured her. I had soup and blackberry tea.

"Do you live with your boyfriend?" I asked when we had found a table. "I mean, the guy who supports you?" I had visions of some broker or bank president who'd set her up in a little love nest, complete with red velvet walls, a white shag rug and a heart-shaped bed. Probably a friend of her father's who was married and had three children.

Trish had removed her coat but not her hat, and she was gobbling her sandwich as if she hadn't eaten for weeks. "Oh no," she said. "We're both very independent. He's an artist and photographer and he has the most fantastic studio, you should see it. It's in Belltown, you know, where all the artists live and it looks right out over the water. He's built a loft in it — it's so cool. You go up a little ladder, and there you are, way up high, and you can look out the window and see the ferries at night — they're so pretty when they're lit up."

"But you don't usually stay there?"

"Nooo, well of course, a *lot*. The thing is, he has to be alone really a lot, to do his work."

"So he's a photographer. What's his name?"

Trish ignored the question. "He's not just a photographer," she said, starting on the mocha-almond torte. "He does all kinds of art — xerox art and collages and sometimes really big paintings. Like, before I knew him I didn't know anything about art. I thought art was like," she thought hard a moment, "like art in my parents' house, like" she searched for a name, "Picasso or something."

"Your parents have a Picasso?"

"Well, no, but you know, *like* that. Museum-type stuff."

"And he supports you, this artist?"

She nodded, almost too quickly. "He gives me anything I want — clothes and... And we eat out a lot. And he's taught me so much. I mean, here I was in school — in this really good girls' school — and I just hadn't learned a thing. I mean, sure, *dates* and algebra and history and *grammar*, but nothing important!"

She seemed intent on convincing me. "And he loves me, he loves me so much, that's what I can't get over. Because I never had that at home. It was Dad working all the time at the office and Mom giving parties. Sure we had money! But we didn't have love!"

It all sounded as if she'd read it somewhere — more likely, heard it said in an old movie, a very old movie. I almost laughed. But if there was anything I remembered from my adolescence, it was that I had hated being laughed at, especially when I was baring my soul.

Trish's sincerity, real or not, hadn't interfered with her appetite, however. She had polished off the torte and was pressing the moist crumbs to her small rosebud mouth with a purple fingernail.

"These slices are so small," I said. "Have another one. On me, of course." I handed her a couple of dollars.

She hesitated a moment. "I feel so stupid leaving my wallet at home. My boyfriend gave me two hundred dollars yesterday and it's just sitting there." But she took the two bills.

I watched her walk quickly back into line, tall and thin, with those spindly limbs and big breasts. She moved her body not with the unconscious grace girls sometimes have, when they're experiencing that strange new power to attract, but with an unwilling, almost contemptuous severity, as if she were saying, "Yes, look all you want. Assholes!"

And look they did. Every male eye in the place was riveted on her as she paraded back with her second dessert. But if she didn't want them to look, why did she wear those tight jeans and high-heeled boots? Wrong, Nilsen, I told myself. Not everybody wants to look like you do. And I flushed a little as I glanced down at my own worn turtleneck sweater and overalls. Like most feminists I'd probably say I dressed this way to be comfortable and free. In truth I was dressed partly for protection, like a soldier who dons a chemical warfare uniform before venturing into enemy territory.

But if I were free to wear anything I wanted to . . . That was stupid. I *was* free, freer than I acted anyway. I just didn't like to go shopping.

Trish polished off her second slice of torte with almost as much relish as she had the first, then lit a Marlboro and blew smoke out her sharp little nose.

"I'm going to have to get back to work soon," I told her. "So maybe we could talk a little about how to help you — I mean, what I can do."

"Wait," she said, sounding almost panic-stricken, as if I were forcing her to remember a bad dream she'd almost put out of her mind. "You don't have to go back so soon, do you? We just got here."

"I'm afraid I do. June's all alone, unless Carole has come. But you can come back with me if you want. If that makes you feel . . ." I was going to say "safer," struck by her look of fear, but instead said, "better."

"It's just that — I don't feel like being at home today. I mean, after last night. Rosalie and me, well, we were sort of roommates — when I wasn't at my boyfriend's."

"She was really a good friend of yours then."

"We hung out together almost every day. She was really fun to be around. She was always laughing and cracking jokes. We thought maybe we would go on a trip together — she kept wanting to go back to California where she was from. I've never been there. I've never been anywhere except to Portland where my dad . . ." she broke and continued nervously, "Rosalie was always making jokes about the weather here. She used to say she was losing her tan!" Trish giggled. "Isn't that a riot? She always said things like that."

"You say your dad lives in Portland?"

"No, I mean, he has business there, so we sometimes went down there." She looked uncomfortable and I let it go. There were a lot of mysteries about Trish and I'd already begun to suspect that there were many things in her life she was lying about. A rip-off artist, a street-wise hooker, that's what June had said she was. I'd have to be careful. But there was something in Trish I liked and something, too, I felt called upon to protect.

"Why don't you just hang out at the shop this afternoon? We'll go upstairs and I'll buy you a book and you can read and do whatever you want and then I'll take you home to my house for dinner. And we can have a good long talk then."

She looked as if she'd been given a present. Or a life raft. "Oh, that would be great!"

We went upstairs and I bought her *Jane Eyre*. She might as well start at the beginning.

7

CAROLE WAS TALKING on the phone when we came back and waved while continuing her story.

"So then he asked me was I an arsonist and where had I gotten that blow torch anyway. I was only trying to help, I said, am I supposed to wait for the weather to warm up so I can wash my dishes? I mean, I don't feel like doing my dishes every day, so when I *do* feel like it I can't stand something like the stupid weather and then the stupid landlord saying I can't.

"Getting off in a minute," she mouthed to me, and pointed vigorously at the receiver, to indicate the other person was talking too much.

Carole had short straight blond hair that stood up surprised above her forehead with one lock that trailed down in a long curl like a question mark behind her left ear. She had eager, slightly empty blue eyes below startled brows and a gaze with the weak intensity of a flashlight turning here and there in a dark room full of strange furniture.

"Well, I'm not a firebug, if that's what he thinks," she announced when she'd hung up the phone and turned to us with her

30

charming, slightly wacky smile.

"Who, your landlord?" I asked. I always found myself trying to clarify the direct antecedents of Carole's pronouns.

"Really! So who's this?"

I introduced Trish.

"I love your sweatshirt," Carole said warmly. She herself was dressed in a training suit as usual. Besides taking aerobics and self-defense she had lately started running three miles a day and was forever doing stretches in the front office and bounding from one room to the next, singing snatches of Chuck Berry and Cyndi Lauper.

I wondered once more what it would be like to go to bed with her. Her attitude towards me was eager and flirtatious, not seductive, but vaguely unsettling. She had a way of standing stock-still when I was talking to her, eyes wide, lips parted, quivering slightly like an ardent, but well-trained retriever longing to put her paws on my shoulders and lick my face.

I was probably just imagining it.

"Well, back to the grinding board," Carole said and sprang away to the darkroom, accompanying herself with "Maybelline" ("Why don't you be true?").

Trish watched her leave. "Is it just women who work here?"

"Mostly," I said. "There's one guy, Ray. He's in Nicaragua now with my sister. She's my twin."

"Wow, does she look like you?"

"She used to. We seem to get less alike every year. Age, I guess."

"You don't have so many wrinkles though," Trish said innocently. "Just around your eyes."

"Well, I'm only thirty." I might as well have said one hundred thirty.

"Wow," she said. "I never would have guessed."

The afternoon passed quickly. Once people dug out from the snow and their childhood memories, they wanted to get back to work. January might be regarded as a slow month overall in the printing trade, but we always had our regulars. The newsletters and flyers for mailings, here and there a poster or brochure.

June always left at four-thirty to pick up her kids. Carole was supposed to stay till five-fifteen, but these days she was usually out the door by five at the latest. "It's something psychological about the darkness," she'd said, pulling down her eyebrows to show she was serious. "When it gets dark I need to get home and build a fire. It's the cavewoman instinct, I guess."

Like me, Carole lived alone now. She'd moved out of her lesbian household at the beginning of December, to a little house out in the North End.

"I'll have a garden and fruit trees in the summer," she'd exulted. "Space, space, I needed space. And I *really* needed to get some *privacy.*"

That I understood. When I'd moved out of my own collective household last summer I'd been wild with delight at first. I could put up anything on my walls, play any music I liked, any time I wanted, cook anything or nothing—and nobody was going to remark on it or offer their opinion. Nobody was going to complain if there was a hair in the bathroom sink or the garbage was too full when it was my day to clean the kitchen. There was going to be absolutely *no discussion* when I threw the newspaper on the floor after reading it or left a pan in the sink to soak for a week.

But such pleasures, while long overdue, had in the end proved strangely trivial and unsatisfying. I'd often found myself staying late at the shop, hoping for an invitation to dinner from June or Penny, postponing the moment when I'd have to face the emptiness of my apartment, and of its secret heart—the refrigerator.

Tonight, at least, I'd cook something decent. When June left at four thirty and Carole shortly after, humming a little apologetic tune about her frozen pipes, so did Trish and I. We took the Number 7 trolley up to the Broadway QFC and I bought cannelloni shells, ricotta and mozzarella, parsley, black olives and a Rioja wine. I still had some good tomato sauce around; Andrea, the baker, had also outfitted me with a winter's supply of home-canned jars of preserves and sauces.

Trish asked if we could get some Diet Pepsi too and have ice cream for dessert, and got me to buy her another pack of Marlboros. She said she liked any food that wasn't green and that she would probably like cannelloni, since she'd always liked spaghetti.

The sadness of an early violet twilight had turned festive on Broadway, now that it was truly dark and the street lit up. Most of the snow was gone from the sidewalks, but the taste of it lingered in the air, crisp and biting. Voices of shoppers and people coming home from work rang out, as if sound and air had both become solid objects, creating friction where they met.

"Oh, a kitty!" said Trish happily as Ernesto lumbered out of the bedroom. "Wow, he's big, isn't he?"

"Big, mean and ugly."

"No, he's not — are you, little kitty cat? You're *sweet*!"

Ernesto was purring madly and running around her spike-heeled boots, rubbing himself against them. Then he rolled over on his back with his huge paws in the air and looked at Trish adoringly. She got down on her hands and knees, still in her coat and hat, and scratched his belly. "Yes, he's such a good baby, isn't he?"

"Do you have any animals?" I asked.

She shook her head. "I had a dog once but they put it to sleep . . . I'd like a kitty. How long have you had this one?"

"Two days. I'm cat-sitting for a friend." I went into the kitchen and started unpacking the groceries. From the living room I heard, "Then you're all alone in the world, aren't you, kitty cat?"

"He's got me," I called back, slightly miffed. Maybe I hadn't tried hard enough with Ernesto.

I put water on to boil for the canelloni shells and began to mix the stuffing of ricotta and mozzarella together with chopped parsley and olives. I opened the bottle of Rioja and poured myself a glass, then poured some Diet Pepsi for Trish. Horrible stuff, it fizzed like watery brown sewage that had been treated with strong chemicals.

Trish was tip-toeing around my apartment. I could hear June's voice — or was it Penny's? — in my head: "She's probably casing the joint. And tonight, after you're asleep, her boyfriend, a criminal with a string of convictions for breaking and entering will come in and steal your . . ." My what? My 1966 Hermes typewriter? My Sony cassette player with one speaker dead? My Canon camera, made for five dollars in Korea and sold for seventy-five? It was broken now and I had been debating whether or not to get it fixed, because one hour of American labor was forty-five dollars and the shop had suggested I just get a new one. Trish's criminal friend was welcome to it — and to the stupid car, too. I'd leave the keys out.

33

Trish came into the kitchen, still wearing her coat and hat, as if she'd be ready to leave at any point if asked.

"I know you don't eat green things," I said. "But I'm just throwing a little parsley in for color. Parsley's a good introduction to vegetables. It's sort of like water — it has almost no taste."

She laughed a little and sat down at the kitchen table and sipped at her Diet Pepsi. Whenever she sat she looked smaller and more vulnerable. Her shoulders tended to hunch and in the trench coat her breasts weren't noticeable. After a moment she took off her black felt hat and laid it on a chair. The frosted ash-blond hair was flattened at the crown and clung to the sides of her triangular face. She looked suddenly tired and much younger. When Ernesto came in, for the first time he didn't go straight to his food dish, but jumped up on Trish's lap. She cuddled him lovingly but not with the same kind of attention as before. She seemed absent-minded, thinking of something else.

I kept up a lively chatter while I prepared the food. I told her about how Penny and I had inherited the print shop after our parents died, and how we struggled to keep it going. I told her about June and Penny and their women's skydiving club and how June was always after me to try it. Trish listened and laughed from time to time. I interrupted myself once to ask if she'd like to make a phone call or anything, let anyone know she was here, anyone who might be worried . . . but she shook her head.

After a little while, when the cannelloni was safely in the oven, and I was cleaning up the sink, she suddenly said,

"Do you have a boyfriend?"

The question caught me by surprise and I started to mumble no, but then I braced myself against the sideboard, turned and said, "I'm a lesbian."

"That's what I thought."

"What tipped you off? My short hair, my overalls?"

"No, it's how you walk. How you just *are*," she said and added, "Rosalie was a lesbian too. But I'm not."

"But surely you don't think . . ." I took off my glasses and polished them nervously, aghast at the mere suggestion of being thought an elderly predator.

"I just like people to know where I stand," she said. Her wise tone was at such variance with her childish face that I couldn't help laughing.

"For such a young person you seem to have some very decided ideas where you stand. Clearly against vegetables and for Diet Pepsi, for instance. Anyway," I continued lightly, determined to pass it off as a joke, "You're not my type. And besides, what makes you think I don't have a *girlfriend*?"

"Because you seem lonely," she said matter-of-factly, and stroked Ernesto.

"You're a psychologist already then?"

"When you're out on the street and doing dates you get to know a lot about people," she said. "And you can feel it, feel their loneliness coming off them—like something cold, like cold mist or steam."

"You know a lot for being only seventeen going on eighteen," I said. I didn't pick up then on the part about the street and dates; I was busy resisting the picture of myself as a block of dry ice, sending up clouds of angst. "Are you sure you're not forty-five?"

"Sometimes I feel older than I am," she said, not looking at me. "Sometimes I don't even remember how old I am—I've lied about it so often. And I can hardly remember when I was little—it seems like such a long time ago."

"How old are you really, Trish?"

"Fifteen," she said, and added hopefully, "Sixteen next summer."

8

O<small>H</small>," I SAID, RATHER LAMELY. "Does your boyfriend know?"

"Oh, sure," Trish said and then, flippantly, "He likes it — as long as I act grown-up."

"That must be a strain sometimes."

"Not really." She lit another Marlboro as if to prove her point. "See, I really love him. I just — feel different when I'm around him. Like there are just the two of us in the world." She dragged and blew smoke out, intense but distant. "I'd do anything for him. And he'd do anything for me. He'd do anything for me," she repeated and seemed to lose her train of thought.

I took a peek at the cannelloni. It was starting to bubble at the edges.

"But you see other men, right?" I didn't know how to put it. "I mean, your 'dates'?"

"I don't take it personally. It's their problem. Men don't care about anything else. Why shouldn't I get paid for it?" She reeled off the reasons flatly, then was silent, petting Ernesto. "The dates don't have anything to do with being in love with Wayne. He and I don't even have sex!" She said this triumphantly, but there was aversion in her voice as she continued, "I don't like sex that much. And when I like a person I don't want sex to have anything to do with it."

Trish looked at me. "I slept with Rosalie. But we didn't do anything. Just hugged and stuff."

I was having trouble figuring out how the boyfriend came into all this.

"How did you meet Wayne?"

She seemed disconcerted. "Did I tell you his name?"

"Just his first name, don't worry."

"I don't care, but it's so unfair — when a girl has a boyfriend and she does dates, that the police can arrest *him*..."

"But I thought he supported you?"

"He does, he does, he gives me anything I want. I told you he's an artist. Once he sold a painting and he took me out to eat at the Four Seasons. Oh, it was so fun, getting all dressed up and wearing a fur coat and Wayne wore a tuxedo and rented a limousine. Wayne is so great like that. He likes to do things to surprise me — send me flowers or drive somewhere we've never been. And he's got such a cool studio, did I tell you, with paintings hanging all over the walls. I really like his friends too, they're so interesting. One guy named Karl has this long beard and no hair on his head and he always wears black. Karl's really a great painter, Wayne says, but he won't sell his paintings because he thinks people won't understand them."

I took the cannelloni out of the oven, feeling as if I were listening to a program on the Abstract Expressionists of the fifties. Misunderstood bald artists and impressionable young girls — thirty years later had anything really changed?

"Sure you won't try the salad? It's just lettuce and tomatoes and green peppers."

"I could eat the tomatoes, I guess, but not if they have any stuff on them already, that oil and vinegar stuff. I just eat Thousand Island dressing."

"Well, you're out of luck," I said, not sure whether to be irritated or amused. "I *don't* eat Thousand Island dressing and there's none in my house."

"Do you like to live alone?" she asked, as I was dishing out the cannelloni. She had kept Ernesto on her lap, and his squarish, tufty head kept appearing over the top of the table like a tea cozy.

"It has its ups and downs," I said. "Your social life needs more organization. If you live in a collective household you can all be sitting around and someone will say, hey, let's go to the midnight movie, and you'll all go. But if you live alone you're always having to call around and if you do find someone who's home, chances are they'll look in their appointment book and say, 'I have a free hour Thursday, three weeks from now.'"

Trish took this in without laughing, as I'd meant her to, and dug into her cannelloni. "What happened to your last girlfriend?"

I could have told her about Dandi, Betty, Andrea or Devlin. I could have mentioned my on and off attraction to Carole. Instead I said, "She went away last summer. First from me and then from Seattle. I still think about her."

"What was her name?"

"Hadley." It was strange that I still felt like smiling when I said it. She treated you *bad*, girl, I reminded myself firmly.

"Rosalie had a girlfriend when she came up to Seattle. They came up together. The girlfriend was white; her name was Karen."

"What happened?"

"Oh, they had a fight and Karen split."

"Do you still see her? Maybe she knows something about . . ."

"No, she went back to California, I guess. She just disappeared."

The words hung a little longer in the air than they were meant to.

"So Rosalie was living alone?"

"Yeah—in this hotel downtown. She had a little room she'd fixed up pretty nice with a couple of posters and a lot of plants. She really loved plants, especially cactus, because it reminded her of the desert and California and everything. She was always getting a new little plant and putting it in the window. She called them her babies, she used to talk to them, like, 'Hi, how ya doing?' every morning to each of them, she said she'd read somewhere they liked it, that it made them grow. It wasn't weird though—it was funny. I liked waking up in the morning and hearing her."

"You used to stay with her a lot then?"

Trish nodded. She finished her first helping of cannelloni and seemed to like it well enough to reach for more. "Yeah, I went back last night. But it was too strange, thinking of Rosalie never coming home again and the little cactuses all sitting there in a row."

"Where are you going to stay now? With Wayne?"

She suddenly seemed to lose interest in her food. She pushed her plate away and resumed stroking Ernesto. "No," she said slowly.

"You're welcome to stay here for a while," I said. "You can sleep on the sofa bed."

"You mean that?" She gave a little jump and Ernesto, surprised, thudded off her lap. "Oh, I knew you were a nice person when you picked me up. I was so glad it was a lady. I couldn't have stood to be in a car with a guy."

"Do you want to talk about it, tell me what happened? Are you still afraid — of being recognized by the person who did it?"

I saw from her eyes she was. But also that she didn't trust me enough.

"You know," she said, with self-conscious pathos, "I'm really tired, I feel like I could just fall asleep right now."

I didn't press her further, though I wish I had. I cleared the plates from the table. "You'd probably like a bath too."

"Would I! I feel filthy."

I ran the water and gave her a towel, then made up the couch into a bed and found her a clean flannel nightgown.

When she came back into the living room after her bath, she finally looked her true age — makeup gone, hair flat and wet, woman's body hidden in the ballooning flannel gown, barefoot.

She went over to the sofa bed and then turned hesitantly to face me. "You can sleep with me if you want."

"You're here as my guest. And it doesn't cost anything. Now good-night. And sleep well."

Christ, I thought. What have they done to this kid?

An hour later I peeked in to check on her. She was fast asleep, one arm thrown up to her forehead in a nocturnal parody of the distressed damsel, the other firmly around Ernesto, who opened up one eye to glare at me and then closed it again.

9

HOW OLD WERE YOU when you quit school?" I asked Trish the next morning. We were back at the table, eating breakfast, a meal which, happily, she seemed to have no reservations about, perhaps because its main colors were cheerful shades of yellow, red and brown.

"I was in the ninth grade, I must have been fourteen, cause it was last year." She took a large bite of toast spread with raspberry preserves. "Mmmm, I had one teacher I liked, that was my English teacher, Mrs. Horowitz—she used to tell me books to read and sometimes give them to me, like Hemingway and Steinbeck. I liked him a lot, I read a lot of what he wrote."

"Aside from English, though, you didn't like school all that much?"

"I liked it all right in elementary school," Trish said, putting another piece of bread in the toaster. "I mean, it was all my friends who went there and we did fun things—and at first I thought it was cool to go to Junior High—have different teachers for different subjects and all that—but then, I don't know, I just kind of lost interest. I guess when I met Wayne I lost interest. I mean, he was talking about things on a whole different level."

As always when she talked about Wayne, her eyes took on a protective, wary cast.

"What was all that about a private girls' school?"

"I thought it sounded better." She looked uneasy. "I mean, people like you better if they think you're smart and rich."

"And your parents—do they really live in Broadmoor?"

"Why do you want to know all this stuff about me?" She was suddenly, surprisingly hostile. "What's any of it to you?"

I thought of snapping back, You came to me, didn't you?, but controlled myself. "Okay, you ask me some questions about my life. About school, my work, my parents..."

"I'm not interested in your stupid life," she said. Her eyes narrowed and her triangular little face sharpened. She got up to empty the ashtray and didn't come back to the table, but instead wandered about the kitchen and then out to the living room, restless and angry. "Hey Ernesto, here kitty, kitty..."

"Adults think they know everything," she suddenly shouted from where I couldn't see her. "They think they can just ask you anything about your life and then they can tell you what they think of it and what you should do. Like they don't have any problems themselves."

"You think I don't have any problems? I have problems, a lot of problems." I still couldn't see her and raised my voice.

"Yeah, but they're adult problems like work and things," she called back.

"They're not adult problems." I went to the kitchen door and looked at her. She was back in the sofa bed, curled up with Ernesto. "They're human problems—like loneliness and losing people or being away from people you care about."

"Well, you've got your sister anyway, your twin sister," she muttered, not looking at me. "I don't have any real brothers and sisters at all."

It was strange how quickly I descended to her level. I almost countered, Well, I don't have any parents, so there! But I stopped myself in time.

"You seem kind of jumpy this morning," I said instead. For the first time it occurred to me that she might have a habit, might be needing a fix. Under the nightgown her broad shoulders seemed to be shaking.

41

She said something unintelligible, her face buried in Ernesto's fur. I went into my bedroom and started to get dressed.

After a few minutes she asked in a high and cheerful voice if I was leaving for work soon.

I had misgivings about leaving her in my apartment alone, but I did have to go to work and didn't want to put her back out on the street without learning more about her and Rosalie. I came back to the living room and started explaining things about the heating and the stove and the faucet leak in the bathroom.

Her bad humor seemed to have vanished as quickly as it had come and she was eager to appear a responsible guest.

"There's not a lot of food here, unless you want to eat the cannelloni, so you may want to go out. I'll leave you some money. If you wanted, you could come down to the shop and we could eat lunch together. You want to do that?"

"I'll think about it," she said. "Maybe I'll just stay here and read *Jane Eyre*. I could call you if I'm coming."

"You're sure there's nobody you want to contact—like..." I didn't want to mention her parents and get her angry again, "like a friend or someone? Just to let them know where you are?"

"Not really. Oh, I might call Wayne just to say hi, but it's no big deal. We don't check up on each other."

"Okay then. Well, give me a call if you want to come for lunch. Otherwise I'll be back around five-thirty or six. Here's the shop's number."

I felt dissatisfied and full of questions, both about her and about my own course of conduct. There'd been a murder after all and Trish might be the only witness. Should I call the police, even if she'd asked me not to? I wanted to treat her as an equal, but I knew she was still a child. What if her parents were looking for her—and if they weren't they should be—and what was my responsibility to them? Should I try to call them, just to let them know Trish was safe? I didn't even know Trish's last name—and I didn't know how to ask without sounding suspicious.

"I'll be fine here," she reassured me brightly, as if guessing my worries. "Me and Ernesto, we'll just cuddle up and read."

"You find out anymore about her, this girl you're saving from a life of crime?" June asked. She had found a small item in the

42

newspaper about Rosalie's death, hidden near the real estate ads.

"A few things. She's only fifteen and she doesn't come from Broadmoor."

"See?"

"June," I warned. "You promised. . . It's strange though, she keeps talking about this guy Wayne she's in love with and about how much he loves her and all the money and things he gives her —but it turns out she was practically living with Rosalie and she doesn't seem to want to turn to him for help."

"He's her pimp, that's why! She probably can't show up les she's got her quota."

"What do you mean, her quota?"

"Her money, girl. He tells her she's got to bring in a hundred and fifty—two hundred dollars a day and she's got to make it or she can't show her face."

"She said he's an artist, a photographer. He's got a studio in Belltown. That doesn't sound like a pimp to me."

"You think pimps are all Black studs driving around in Cadillacs? You've been watching too many Hollywood movies. She on dope?"

I shook my head and then shrugged. "I guess I don't know how to tell," I admitted. "She seemed restless for a while this morning, but she was all right when I left. She got angry pretty fast when I asked her about her parents."

"She'll go out later to score if she needs it," June predicted. "Probably a cokehead if her ole man's an artist. Though kids these days—she could be on anything. The latest thing I heard, they're spraying paint into socks and sniffing it. They go crazy."

"June, would you give her a break? She's only a kid and she's scared out of her wits."

"Humph," said June. "Well, you watch out she doesn't sell out your apartment while you're gone. Seriously."

Carole came in, forty-five minutes late, mumbling something about snow in her driveway and looking totally disheveled.

"Don't suppose you've noticed," said June with a scathing look, "But most of the snow has melted. . . What'd you do, meet another true love of your life?"

"Just get off my case, would you?" Carole lashed out in a rare fit of temper. Her blond hair stood up in furious spikes above her forehead. "There's still snow in the North End and most of it's in

43

my street." She stomped back to the darkroom and called, "Look at my car if you don't believe me!"

"It's true," I reported, peering out the window. "Carole's car has snow on the roof."

"You know something?" June snapped. "You ought to get your own TV show — *Pam Nilsen: Miss Fair Puts In Her Two Cents*. You ought to get a medal for sympathetic remarks."

I sat down on the couch. "Look, all right, June — we both miss Penny and Ray. But wishing isn't going to bring them back. We've got six weeks and if we don't all start getting along better here we might as well cash it in right now and fly on down to Nicaragua to join them."

I'd never seen June cry before and I didn't see her now either, but sudden tears came into her bright brown eyes and she let out her breath with a big huff. "You're right, I guess. It's not Ray so much though, it's Penny. Only two days and I miss her," she finally said. "It seems so — empty — around here."

"It doesn't have to be that tough, does it? Listen, what are you and the girls doing this weekend? You want to go to the zoo or something?"

"Change that show to *Pam Nilsen: Social Director*," she said, but she smiled this time. "I've got me a boyfriend and two kids, so what am I feeling so abandoned for? Anyway, I'm going sky-diving with my club on Saturday. That's something you should check out. We've got an extra parachute."

"Hey, I'm talking giraffes and you're talking broken bones."

"Just come up in the plane. Do you good to get your feet off the ground for once."

And to my alarm, I said I would.

10

IRISH DIDN'T COME BY FOR LUNCH and she didn't call either. Neither of which worried me all that much. I tried calling her twice in the afternoon, but there no answer both times. That worried me a little more.

I kept my fears to myself, however, and put my energy into attempting to bring a bit of peace and harmony into the workplace. I went into the darkroom and got Carole talking about her frozen pipes and unplowed street, until she too began to unthaw a little. I asked if she'd like to have dinner with me and June at my house Sunday night. At first she seemed distant and glum, but by the end of the conversation she was more her old self and thanked me profusely for inviting her.

"I'm sorry I was so out of it this morning, Pam," she said, sighing and twisting her long curl between her fingers. "It was Suz, you know, that woman I met at the New Year's party, the one with the cute little tattoo, you know, the anchor? Well, I spent the night with her last night and you know what she did, she brought out a pair of handcuffs. If I hadn't had my blow torch I don't know what I would have done."

For such an innocuous, optimistic person, Carole certainly managed to get herself in some strange situations. But it didn't occur to me to ask her what she was doing with a blow torch at her lover's house. Knowing Carole she probably just forgot she was carrying it.

I went back to the press room and asked June about dinner too. She rolled her eyes and said, "Let's not carry this collective friendliness too far."

"Oh, come on, June, it won't kill you. Carole's not that bad. *I* think she's funny."

"Yeah and so is Lucille Ball. For about two minutes."

"But she means well — she's just a little . . ."

"Cuckoo." June sighed, "Yeah, all right. You want me to bring something?"

"Just yourself. I'll make something good." It would be my big chance to move into the Main Entries section of my cookbook.

Mission accomplished, I turned to my work in the front office, trying to understand Penny's instructions about the bookkeeping. It *did* feel lonely without Penny and Ray around, as if we were acting in a play with only half the characters, but I told myself it was for the best: Nicaragua had two willing workers and I didn't have my sister suggesting that I might be getting in over my head with Trish and her problems.

The afternoon was cold and quiet. Andrea called once and asked rather pathetically if I'd enjoyed the fruitcake she'd left outside my door for Christmas. I didn't tell her that I'd had to give it away, finding myself shy of a suitable gift for someone else at the last minute — but I did praise the tomato sauce I'd used on the cannelloni last night.

"I have some really great prune and apple chutney I could give you . . . you want to go to a movie or play this weekend?"

"Uh, that's really nice, Andrea, but, um, I'm really busy these days."

"Oh, sure, I understand," she murmured sadly. "You've probably got someone new, haven't you?"

"Well, kind of."

Sometimes I wished Andrea and Devlin and the rest of them could get together and tell Hadley what she was missing.

*

Shortly before I closed up the shop at five I tried calling Trish again. The line was busy, an irritating but still reassuring sound that made me feel a little like the mother of a teenager. Yet I found myself oddly happy too, knowing that she was there, that there was someone waiting for me at home. It enlivened my spirits and quickened my appetite. I'd go by the Market on the way home and pick up something special for us tonight – fresh shrimps in their shells sounded good – or would Trish think they were too icky?

I went down to First and caught a bus that let me off at the far corner of the Market, by DeLaurenti's. I'd decided after all to stick with pasta and bought tortellini and sun-dried tomatoes, Nicoise olives and a hunk of Romano cheese. At the vegetable stands I bought Romaine lettuce, a cucumber and red bell peppers, along with some tiny sweet Satsuma oranges. I stopped to goggle over the headlines at the Read All About It newsstand. MOTHER DELIVERS ALIEN BABY: HUSBAND DEMANDS DIVORCE blared the *National Enquirer*, while *Business Week* worried over the Japanese: SAMURI AND COWBOYS: SHOW-DOWN AT THE IMPORT CORRAL. I noticed the stand was starting to carry *La Barricada*, the Sandinista paper, and bought a copy, more out of a sudden longing to participate in whatever my sister might be experiencing down there than because I expected my Spanish to be up to reading it.

It was cold out; much of the snow had melted, but the air was frosty. People in down parkas and long wool coats rushed around making their last-minute purchases, the street musicians played old folk and new reggae and over the whole scene shone the beneficent light of the big red letters: PUBLIC MARKET CENTER. The words gave everything a festive, incandescent glow, gleaming on the worn brick of the street and enclosing the stage-like setting within a frame of color. For a moment, while I waited for the traffic light to change on First, I was stopped by the magic of it, the sense that here was the heart of the city, here was the city's heart, beating red and warm against the cold black sky.

Then I crossed the street and immediately everything changed. The street kids were lined up outside the boarded-up, grafitti-covered windows of the abandoned building that had been J.C. Penney's Department Store all through my childhood. Another group stood in front of the Son Shine Inn opposite. The inn was run by the Union Gospel Mission and displayed a faded painting of Jesus holding out his hands. Bedraggled looking street people went in and out; I guessed the Christians must be serving dinner inside. Outside its door a steady contingent of kids hung out, managing to look both restless and bored. They played with each other's hair, pushed and jabbed and hugged each other's bodies. A couple of the boys, Black and white, had ghetto blasters; they held on to them proprietarily or swung them like playful weapons at each other. Sound enveloped each boy and his circle, and fought with the music of his rival. "Hey, baby, what's happening?" the boys called to the girls, who giggled and pretended to run away. "Nothin' man, not a thing."

It wasn't exactly Times Square; one seedy block didn't qualify as a lurid red-light district. It was more like an urban shopping mall somehow, where the boys strutted and the girls combed their hair. The difference was only that most of these kids didn't go home at night.

I waited for the Number 7 trolley in front of the Pay 'n Save. The spirit of the city's evening no longer seemed quite as festive, in spite of all the nicely dressed people around, going home a little late from work with packages and bags in their gloved hands. I kept seeing drunks in frayed sweaters, bag ladies pushing shopping carts, crazy people, beggars and kids with nowhere to go. It was as if there were two paintings, one on top of the other. And the one on top, the slick attractive one with the good-looking, youngish, employed shoppers, was peeling and cracking, so that the bottom painting was showing through, a faded, miserably drawn fresco that looked like it depicted people from another century.

I got on the trolley, feeling shaken, found a seat, and kept my eyes closed nearly all the way home.

Ernesto was mewing loudly when I opened the door.

"Trish?" I called cautiously. "Trish?"

The lights were all on, in the bedroom and kitchen as well as the living room. The sofa bed had been folded back up and the flannel nightgown was tucked neatly away under one of the pillows. *Jane Eyre* was open with the spine up. I mechanically picked it up and closed it, using a piece of scribbled paper as a book-mark, noting that Jane was now at Mr. Rochester's house, won-dering what those strange sounds from the attic could be.

"Trish," I called half-heartedly one more time, but I knew she wasn't here.

I picked up *Jane Eyre* again and looked at the scrap of paper inside.

"Dear Pam, I've gone out for a little while, don't worry. See you later. Trish."

Had she gone out to score drugs or to meet Wayne or to turn a few tricks? Who had she been talking to on the phone? Had any-one else been here, had they taken her away against her will?

There was no sign of a struggle, as they say in mysteries. There was no sign of anything at all except this note.

"Do you think she'll come back?" I asked Ernesto. "Do you think she's all right?"

He sat on his haunches and stared at me accusingly.

"I never should have left her alone without finding out who she's afraid of."

And Ernesto yowled to show he agreed.

11

I WAITED UNTIL ABOUT NINE, hoping that Trish might show up. When I wasn't pacing the floor I was watching the phone. I ate some of the cannelloni left from the night before; I didn't have much interest in cooking. Once the phone rang, but it was only Betty, the classical guitarist, who had an extra ticket to Julian Bream at the Opera House in February. Would I like to go? I decided that February was far enough away to say yes to anything; besides, it showed that Betty no longer had any immediate designs on me and really did want to be friends.

I also thought about calling June, but I was afraid she might not give me either the sympathy or the advice I wanted. If my car were broken down she'd be the first person to help; I wasn't so sure about her when it came to emotional support. She'd probably tell me I could have expected it, which wasn't what I needed to hear, and recommend a good movie on TV. There was always Carole; she had a good heart — and a blow torch — but it was hard to know how reliable she'd be as a sidekick.

Around eight-forty-five I looked in the Yellow Pages under professional photographers for anyone with the first name of

Wayne, but didn't find a single one. Not that I really thought I would. This so-called artist lover of Trish's sounded faker than a xerox copy to me. She said she loved him — what did she know about love!

Suddenly I put on my jacket and yellow-striped cap, my blue muffler and mittens, and went out again. I thought about taking my car, but still couldn't face the dried blood in the back seat. Instead I walked up to Broadway and got on the Number 7 again.

Four hours had made a difference. The Market and shops were closed; street life had taken over on Pike. I recognized some of the same kids from earlier; many were high now, running back and forth across the street, sharing cigarettes, talking in loud, excited voices.

I went up to one of the girls, a quiet looking thing of thirteen or fourteen, standing on the edge of a crowd, not sure whether she fit in or not, but determined to look as if she did. She was smoking in small, furtive gestures and was hardly made-up at all. Like Trish she wore a black felt hat; maybe that's why I approached her first.

I touched her shoulder. "Excuse me?"

She jerked around and her eyes widened when she saw me. "Yeah?" she said, trying to be tough. She didn't want any of the others to think I knew her or anything for godssakes.

"I'm looking for a...friend of mine," I said. "I wonder if you know her? Her name's Trish."

The girl stared coolly. "Trish what?"

I tried to act tough as well. "She goes by a lot of different last names."

The girl shrugged and moved in closer to the others. I thought for a minute she was going to ask her friends if they knew, but then I realized she was ignoring me.

"Please," I said, in a low and urgent voice. "It's important that I talk to her. You must know her or where I can find her. She's tall and has streaked blond hair and she wears a black hat like yours. She had a friend named Rosalie."

I discovered the whole group was listening. Another girl, older and harder-looking, with a small rosebud tatoo next to her left eye, said, "We don't know nobody named Rosalie." And with that they all dispersed, simply swam away like a school of disturbed fish, to other parts of the street.

Great, now I'd really blown it. They had probably been asked about Rosalie by the cops; they probably thought I was a cop myself. And the way news spread on the street, nobody was going to give me information. I could see members of the group floating warily about, tipping the others off.

I leaned against the wall of the abandoned department store and thought about what to do next. I could hit some bars in Belltown, the ones where artists hung out; maybe someone would know Wayne. But the thought didn't appeal to me much. Whoever and whatever Wayne was, he had a hold on Trish; he probably wouldn't like the idea of me looking for her one bit. Especially if he was the one who'd gotten her out of my apartment.

I stood there for a while and watched. Near me was a seasoned older girl instructing a younger one to keep off her turf; a crazy-looking boy in a leather vest and T-shirt was yelling he was going to kill the next guy who stole his hat. Among the kids walked a couple of older prostitutes, arm in arm, tight skirts twitching over round asses; a man in a white suit and cowboy hat followed them drunkenly. On the corner was a tall thin guy in a sweater and corduroy coat talking earnestly to a lethargic girl in a pink sweatshirt and pants; he'd taken her by the arm and was showing her a pamphlet. He must be on the Lord's business—she looked too dazed to protest.

I stood there and for some reason began to remember an Introduction to Anthropology class I'd taken as a sophomore at the U. It had been a reassuring thing to hear, at twenty, that your own society was a mere episode in millions of years of human history, no better and no worse than countless societies that have existed or will exist. I recalled the kindly expression of Mr. Lieberman as he told us this, and the varying degrees of disbelief—and relief—on my fellow students' faces.

Like some of my classmates I'd dreamed briefly of following a career in anthropology. Find a Polynesian island of my own and chart its kinship systems, bring honor and fame upon the name of Nilsen. I'd be the Ruth Benedict or Margaret Mead of my generation, braving hardship, weird food and malaria to understand just what made those tribal people tick.

But I'd gotten a little bogged down trying to remember the relative skull sizes of the toolmaking Australopithecus and the homo heidelbergensis, and eventually anthropology, like many scholastic obsessions, had died a natural death at the end of the quarter. Besides, there weren't all that many undiscovered Polynesian islands left.

Being on the street, however, brought back memories of Mr. Lieberman and his lectures on society as a cultural organization. "Go downtown," he used to urge us, "and take a look around. You'll be surprised what you see." That was urban anthropology and nobody wanted to do it. What was Seattle compared with Samoa? But now it suddenly occurred to me that that's exactly what I was doing—looking at this society from the outside, with an anthropologist's eye.

And that wasn't necessarily a good thing.

There were things here that I needed to feel as well as witness. The sexual energy, the danger, the excitement. The way the music was bringing back memories of reckless sexy new kinds of feeling. The way the cold air felt like freedom downtown at night.

"I heard you're looking for Trish. Who are you, anyway?"

The voice, woolly with a cold, was harsher than its owner. She had soft, paper white skin and dyed black hair shaved closely at the sides and long on top, falling into her eyes. In spite of her motorcycle jacket and pierced nose, she was very fragile and young-looking; I could have more easily imagined her curled up by the fireplace in a fluffy bathrobe reading fairy tales than out on the street.

"Pam Nilsen," I said and waited.

She looked disconcerted for a moment, then threw back, "Trish doesn't know anyone named Pam."

"She does now. She stayed at my place last night." I didn't go into it. If she knew something she could tell me, but I was starting to realize you didn't get anywhere if you came on too strong.

The girl took out a cigarette and lighter from her pocket and threw a rapid glance at some of her friends across the street. They'd probably appointed her to be the one to check me out. She obviously wanted to look like she had it all under control.

"I knew Rosalie too," I said. "I was the one who took her to the hospital. She and Trish were together out near Sea-Tac when I picked them up."

"I don't know a Rosalie," she snapped, but she was frightened.

"It doesn't sound like the girl had too many pals around here. Now that she's dead anyway. It's a sad thing when people stop caring what happens to their friends."

I said it casually but I watched her reaction under the fall of dyed black hair. She sniffled and blew out smoke. "Why should I trust you?" she finally asked.

"No reason. Just because Trish did, that doesn't mean you have to."

"Look," she said hoarsely. "There's a million cops out tonight, poking their noses into everything, driving by every five minutes —and all because of...because of that girl getting killed. We can't do a damn thing without them picking us up. It's a drag, a fucking drag."

So much for my powers of observation. I'd been out here almost half an hour and I hadn't noticed a single cop. It must be the plainclothes vice squad, obvious to everyone except me, who expected to see the protectors of the peace in regulation blue.

And for the first time it struck me that I wasn't just observing a scene here; I was being observed. The cop and detective from two nights ago had probably driven by me two or three times. And they were probably wondering what a nice girl like me was doing leaning against the wall of an abandoned downtown department store.

I talked fast. "You don't have to believe me, but I wish you would. Trish has been staying at my apartment because she's pretty scared of something or someone. Late this afternoon she wrote me a note saying she'd be back in a little while. Well, she didn't come back and I'm worried about her. I feel like she's in trouble and I want to help her."

For the first time the girl seemed to listen. She cast a brief, anxious glance at her friends. "Ask Beth Linda, she knows Trish. Maybe she can help you," she said rapidly through her stuffed-up nose.

"Beth?" I looked helplessly over at the group. "Can you point her out? Will she talk to me?"

"Beth's not here. She's a *social worker*. At the Rainbow Center over by the bus station, the place we go to get warm and eat and talk and stuff. They're open late. Yeah, go see Beth. But don't tell anyone I told you!"

12

THE RAINBOW CENTER was full of the same sort of kids I'd seen out on the street; some long-haired druggies and some punks with shaved heads and torn T-shirts. There were a lot of gay boys, some of them incredibly femme with red lipstick and bouffant hair. The main room of the converted office building was thick with cigarette smoke and rang with the sound of laughter and shouting; in one corner a video game pinged relentlessly.

I felt my age immediately.

"Hi," said a woman in jeans and a sweater, coming up to me. "Need some help?"

"Does Beth Linda work here?"

"I'll go get her."

After a few minutes a tall woman with solid fat packed around her big frame came into the room and asked what she could do for me. About thirty-seven or eight, she had short strawberry blond hair that dipped into her forthright green eyes. Freckles saved her from looking like she'd seen a little more of life than she wanted to.

"My name's Pam Nilsen. I'm looking for a girl named Trish. I'm

. . . I'm worried about her."

She nodded. "C'mon in back. Coffee or tea?"

She took me to a small office with a couple of ratty armchairs, bulging file cabinets and a desk that looked more like it was used for piling papers on than for working. Over the desk was a poster of a cat lolling on its back that said, "Take It Easy." The walls didn't keep out the sound of the kids.

I had tea. She took her coffee strong and black, and with one of those papery excuses for a cigarette, a Carlton. She was wearing an oversize pink sweater with a cowl collar that came up to her double chin, polyester pants and fluffy pink bedroom slippers.

"My feet swell at the end of the day," she smiled, when she saw me looking at them. She leaned back in her chair.

"Well, I'm not going to let you explain why you're looking for her, and then give you the runaround. I'll tell you right now that I don't know where she is. . . I haven't seen her for a few months. But I'd still like to know what she's up to. I like the girl."

I told Beth the story, from picking Trish and Rosalie up to Trish's note. I had to talk loudly to make myself heard above the uproar in the front room.

Her freckled face was somber. "I can see why you're worried. Especially with Rosalie dying, and all that stuff about the Green River killer. I didn't know her unfortunately, but it's scary. It could have happened to any of the kids."

Beth lit another cigarette. "All I can tell you is what I know about Trish. She dropped in here on and off for three months or so, last summer and fall. You know, we offer counseling and dinners and some medical and educational services, but it's mainly just a place for kids to feel safe. Trish had had a drug problem and she'd been in a treatment program. She was off drugs when I met her and she was in a group for ex-druggies here. The hard thing about these kids is getting them to attend anything on a regular basis—their sense of time, day to day, week to week, is so erratic. And then we had her in a prostitute's group for a while, that's a weekly rap group, and she seemed to be getting a lot out of it. But like I say, it was a problem getting her to come regularly, and a few months ago she dropped out. It's not like we have any hold on her. We couldn't make her come."

"Who has legal responsibility for her? Her parents?"

"No. She was made a ward of the court the third time she was arrested. She's been in foster homes and group homes, she was institutionalized once. It doesn't matter, she just runs. Until the next time she's picked up and put somewhere. Her parents gave her up as 'incorrigible.' The real name for kids like her isn't runaways, it's throwaways."

"What's her background? What are her parents like?"

Beth put her feet up on the desk. They sat there like huge pink bunnies amidst the thicket of papers. "She's got a mother in Seattle who remarried a few years ago. I gather that was the start of the trouble. A twelve-year-old with all the problems that age has anyway — she had the feeling she lost her mother to this guy. I've met both of them. The mother is one of those sweet, helpless women who can be pushed around so easily — and the stepfather is just the guy to do it. Authoritarian, short-sighted, a little stupid. He wanted Trish out of the house and he's not going to take her back. And then there's the stepbrother."

Beth lit another Carlton and dragged at it futilely, trying to get enough tobacco in her lungs to make it worthwhile. The noise outside her office seemed to increase. I heard pushing and shoving and then an adult male voice, "Knock it off. Right now."

"Did she tell you about him? This Wayne?"

"Wayne! But she said he was her boyfriend, not her stepbrother. She said they were in love."

"Yeah, I know that's what she'd like to believe. I never met him, only heard about him, but he sounds like he's really something: good-looking, very controlling, possessive, one of those *guys*."

She didn't say the word with disgust, more with a bitter self-knowledge of the attraction of such men. It sounded like a past attraction.

"I might have had more luck with Trish if it hadn't been for him. A lot of the girls on the street aren't really into prostitution in a big way. They come downtown, running from their parents, looking for drugs and company — and after a few days, when they're hungry and cold and out of cash, one of their new friends tells them where it's at, how easy it is to get into the car with one of the men cruising by. You suck or jerk him off while he drives around the block and there's your twenty bucks. No big deal. It's not usually until the girl's first arrest that she takes on the whore label and starts feeling like that's what she is. And a lot of the girls we can still help at that point, if they get out of the scene in time.

"But someone like Trish, who was turned out by her step-brother and really had to work the streets, well, the chances are slim she's going to leave the life on her own. It's become too much of what she is, and too easy to go back."

"Then Wayne is her pimp?" June was right.

"Oh, he'd be the last one to call himself a pimp. All the same, that's what he is. And not just with Trish. My suspicion is that Rosalie and a couple of other girls are—were—working for him too."

"But doesn't her mother *know*, doesn't she care?"

"She might, if she weren't married to such a jerk. I tried a couple of family counseling sessions. They were a disaster. The step-father interrupted the mom every time she opened her mouth. And Trish didn't say a word."

"I'd like to talk to the parents if I could."

"Sure . . . but don't expect much." Beth flipped through a Rolodex file and carefully wrote out their address. It was in Lake City, near Carole's. About as far away from Broadmoor as you could get.

"How come you haven't asked me why I'm doing all this, why I'm looking for Trish?"

"If I had to ask you that I wouldn't be here. I understand about wanting to help . . ." She paused and lit another Carlton. "I had some . . . trouble too . . . when I was younger. And I guess, if somebody had come looking for me when I was fifteen . . . somebody who seemed like she cared . . . my life might have been a little different. I don't know, but I wish you luck."

"Thanks."

We shook hands and she held mine for a minute longer. "Just one thing. You're taking on a lot if you get involved with Trish and her family. You can't just walk into a person like Trish's life and walk out again. Too many people have done that already. Once she trusts you, if she ever does, you've got a responsibility."

"I'll try to remember that," I said. But I don't think I really understood what she was saying—then.

13

IT WASN'T EASY, but I managed to convince June that the circumstances warranted me taking the next afternoon off from work.

"I just can't believe she left my apartment of her own free will. Her note said she'd see me later."

"That's as good as good-bye to some people. Can't you just accept that the girl's flown the coop — what do you want to get involved with her parents for anyways? Okay, okay," she said, giving in. "It's fine with me. I'll tell Carole you took sick — *if* she ever comes back from lunch."

"Thanks, June. . . just one more thing?"

She looked at me suspiciously. "What's that?"

"Can I use your car?"

"Only if you promise to bring it back without blood all over the seat. I have enough trouble keeping it clean with just the girls and their little candy wrappers."

Before I drove out to Lake City I took the precaution of going home and changing into some other clothes. A clean pair of jeans, a Shetland sweater, a tweed jacket and hoop earrings, all of which I'd inherited from Penny when she went punk. I put some papers in a briefcase and, on impulse, *Jane Eyre*. I also discovered a clipboard in a desk drawer and scribbled a few things on it.

You look like a social worker, I told the mirror, but that was okay — I was hoping to pass myself off as a government researcher. It was the best way I could think of to ask some questions.

Assuming they were the kind of people who would answer them.

Lake City Way is a long ugly street that could have come out of a kit labeled "Anywhere, U.S.A." Block after block of car dealerships, gas stations and fast food restaurants: Kentucky Fried Chicken, Taco Bell, McDonald's — they were all here, in duplicate and triplicate. No wonder Trish didn't like vegetables. If she'd grown up around here she'd probably never even seen one. I turned off at a street above 135th and found the house easily. Nothing special — a low, yellow three-bedroom set back among firs and with a border of clipped rose bushes along the driveway. I parked and went cautiously up the walk, noticing house plants and lace curtains in the windows.

I expected to find Trish's mother, Melanie Hemmings, at home, but it was a man who finally came to the door. He was short with a powerfully built torso and a spreading belly, a beer belly to judge from the Bud in his hand. Not bad looking, in spite of his receding hairline and blond-red beard stubble, but with a hard, unsatisfied look around his mouth. He must be Rob Hemmings, the stepfather.

He didn't say anything, so I started right in, trying to sound as detached and professional as possible.

"I'm looking for Mrs. Hemmings. The Rainbow Center gave me her name and address for a study I'm conducting. Nancy Todd here. National Institute for Research on Delinquent Youth. Is she in?"

"Work," he said briefly and stared at me. I was regretting wearing levis. Brown polyester pants would have been much better. I smiled brightly and waved my clipboard.

"Perhaps *you* would be able to answer a few questions?"

"National Institute for — yeah, come on in. I got nothing better to do this afternoon. It's about Patti, am I right?"

"Ah, Patricia Hemmings, yes, that's who I'm interested in. Sometimes goes by the name Trish?"

"Maybe she does," he said, allowing me to step past him into the hall. "Wouldn't know. Hemmings isn't her last name though. She kept her father's, Margolin."

I pretended to consult my clipboard. "Yes, that's right. You're Robert Hemmings? The girl's stepfather?"

"Rob," he said. "Take your jacket?"

"Thanks but no, this should be brief." I followed him into the living room, where male and female elements warred. On the sofa back and arms, crocheted doilies; over the fireplace a pair of moose antlers; in the magazine rack, *Good Housekeeping* and *Sports Illustrated*. On the teak coffee table, cute little coasters, and next to them, making rings on the wood, beer cans. The television was turned up loudly on a soap. "No, Billy, I won't let you take the blame. I'll tell you the name of the child's *real* father!" Duh-dum sounded the music, piano and a somber violin. Rob turned it off.

"Construction's a little slow this time of year," he said.

"You're a carpenter?"

"Welder. Worked on some of those big buildings down in Seattle." He said it as if it were another city. "Got a back problem right now," he added, easing himself slowly into a vinyl recliner. "Like a beer?"

"Ah, no thanks." Now what? He didn't seem like such a bad guy. I felt a little guilty.

He took a gulp from his can. "Good thing Melanie kept her job at the Bon. Course I've got disability and workman's comp, but it doesn't go very far."

I murmured something sympathetic and wrote down, "Bon Marché Dept. Store" on my clipboard.

"So it's about Patti, is it? Well, I'll tell you, we don't have much to do with her now, haven't for a long time."

"How long has she been away from home?"

"She's always been a troublemaker," snorted Rob. "Said to her mother when we first got together, that girl is going to cause you a mess of problems if you don't watch out. But Melanie wouldn't listen. She'd been raising the girl alone, couldn't see the girl's attitude."

I pretended to write something down. "Stubborn?" I suggested.

61

"The girl needed straightening out and fast. I tried, but I was too late. Girl should have been straightened out a long time ago. She got in with a bad group of kids, hell, you're studying juvenile delinquents—some of them was real delinquents. Drinking, motorcycles, cutting school...."

"She must have been pretty young, twelve or thirteen, when she started to get influenced...?"

"Old enough to get whipped for it—but Melanie wouldn't let me touch her. Not even when we found out she was messing around. That's when this all started."

"You know she's been a...a..."

"Whore? The whole damned neighborhood knew it. Picked up one night down in Seattle—she was still living here then and we were the ones responsible for her. We had to go down to the detention center and get her. I wanted to smack it out of her good and hard, but Melanie was just crying and crying. I told Patti, this happens again and you're on your own. Two weeks later they got her again. They said she had V.D. I told Melanie, we're not going to go get her and if she ever sets foot in this house again, I'm leaving."

Rob had worked himself up to a righteous anger. His face and ears were red enough to light a fire.

"You have a son as well, don't you?" I asked, as dispassionately as I could.

"If Melanie was here she'd tell you he had something to do with Patti going bad, but that's a goddamned lie. Patti's a whore and she's always been a whore and no goddamned social worker is going to put her back in this house—not when there's an innocent little baby on the way."

I was so angry that the words didn't quite sink in. "Trish is pregnant?"

"Melanie is—seven months." He was still fuming about his son though. "I don't pretend to think the boy's perfect. His mom and me was divorced when he was just a baby and she's raised him all screwed up—taking him to Mexico with her and her artsy friends, putting him in private schools and all. And then trying to dump him on me when she got married again. No wonder Wayne don't know how to hold a job. But he's a good kid all the same. I won't hear nothing said against him. He only tried to help Patti—but she wouldn't listen to him either."

62

"Well, thank you," I said and got up. I suddenly couldn't bear to listen to any more, even though I was sure Rob would be able to regale me for hours with details of Trish's troublemaking. He certainly seemed to hate her—and I suddenly wondered if Rob could have been obsessed with Trish in another way? Obsessed enough with her as a whore to follow her, to kill her friend, to kill her?

"What'd you say the name of your institute was? So I can tell Melanie. Something about juvenile delinquents, am I right?"

"That's right," I said. "And you've been *very* helpful. No, I can find my own way out. Thanks so much."

I heard the television roar alive as I left. "Betty, I'm telling you that it doesn't make any difference. I'll always love you, always and forever."

14

I MADE A FEW PHONE CALLS to various personnel departments and discovered that Melanie Hemmings worked at the Bon Marché in the nearby Northgate shopping mall. Hosiery.

I found her straightening striped and patterned kneesocks on tiny hangers. I went over and fingered a couple on sale. Maybe this was all happening in order that I could enlarge my wardrobe. I never went into department stores if I could help it.

"Can I help you?" she asked, with a timid but friendly smile. Like Trish she had a triangular face and widely spaced eyes. She was petite and dark-haired; under a burgundy smock her pregnancy was very apparent.

"I'm Nancy Todd, with the National Institute for Research on Delinquent Youth..." I realized my voice sounded tentative and added firmly, "I've just talked to your husband and wanted to ask you a few questions about your daughter."

Melanie shook her head. Her dark brown hair was thick and cut in a bob with bangs. "I haven't seen her for months, almost a year," she said distantly. "My husband...well...he...we just don't want to see her, that's all."

I nodded and kept my voice neutral. "When did the trouble begin?"

Her hand went to her abdomen and she looked around for escape. If we'd been at her house she would have politely shown me the door.

"She was such a good girl," Melanie finally said, helplessly. "But something changed a few years ago. I didn't recognize her anymore."

"Do you think it had something to do with your marriage?"

She defended him immediately. "Oh no. Rob wanted to be a father to her... He just believes in discipline."

"Did he—punish her?"

Some memory seemed to hurt Melanie; it showed in her eyes. "I told him I thought it wasn't the right way. I never hit her when she was growing up. And she was such a wonderful little girl, it was just her and me for six years, we always got along. But she put up such a fight when I married Rob. He's a good man, he didn't know much about kids, that was all..." Her hand went anxiously to her belly again. "They just got off on the wrong foot. He has a quick temper sometimes, that's all. He doesn't like being talked back to."

"But the real trouble started when your stepson came to stay with you, didn't it? How old was Trish then?" I was unconsciously shifting from researcher to interrogator.

Melanie's face sharpened, just as Trish's did when she was angry. "He *said* he was only going to stay a couple of weeks, just until he got a place of his own, and he was at our house nearly six months, sleeping on the couch and taking over the garage with his loud music and his art stuff. I *told* Rob it wasn't right, to let a thirteen-year-old girl hang around with a nineteen-year-old boy and his friends, but Rob couldn't understand it. I think he felt bad that he'd missed seeing Wayne grow up—he wanted to pretend that he could have this father-son relationship he'd always wanted. He'd sit Wayne down with a beer in front of the television with him so they could watch football and everything—he couldn't see that Wayne was laughing at him, manipulating him. It was Wayne who turned Patti against us, made her laugh at us, at the way we live, the way we *are*."

It was a hard question to ask. "Did Wayne turn Trish—Patti—into a prostitute?"

"I don't know, I don't know anything about it. My little girl! She's a stranger to me," Melanie burst out and then controlled herself. She went over to a skinny little customer lost among the Queen-sized stockings.

I picked out three pairs of kneesocks and decided to buy them. I also wrote out my name and phone number on a slip of paper. When Melanie was finished ringing up her customer I went over to the cash register.

"I'm sorry for upsetting you," I said. "And for lying. I'm not with any institute. My name is Pam Nilsen and I'm a friend of your daughter's. I think she's in trouble and I'm looking for her."

Beneath the fluorescent lights of the store her pointed face went a little pale.

"I shouldn't have told you anything," she said and turned away.

"Please listen. A friend of Trish's died a few days ago and now Trish has disappeared. She could be in danger. If you have any idea where she might be...if you could tell me where to find Wayne..."

It didn't seem to sink in. Melanie was the kind of woman who, threatened by authority, might tell things to a researcher, but not to a friendly stranger.

I put my hand on her arm. "Please don't give up on her," I said. "Someday she's going to need your support very much. Here's my phone number. If you hear anything from her or see her, please give me a call."

Melanie's lower lip trembled. "You didn't say anything about this to my husband, did you? That you were looking for her?"

I shook my head. "As far as he knows, I'm just filling out forms."

"Cause he would kill me, if I got involved with Patti again...."

I waited while she struggled with herself. "If you want to get in touch with Wayne," she finally said. "I know where he is. He's living at the Redmond Apartments, on First Ave, downtown."

"Thanks. Thanks very much."

"I hope she's all right, I hope...but I just don't want to get involved again. I just can't."

15

I⊤ WAS DARK when I went back out into the parking lot, almost six. But there was no hurry—June had generously offered to let me keep the car until tomorrow and had even more generously offered to help me wash out the blood in the Volvo's back seat Saturday morning. On impulse I decided to drive by Carole's house, since I was practically in the neighborhood. I felt a need, after talking with Rob and Melanie, for a reality check, even though I wasn't quite sure Carole could provide it.

Carole's house was just like her, full of projects enthusiastically begun, abandoned and then absent-mindedly displayed. A wall hanging unraveled halfway through its sunset-over-the-mountains' theme; a clay head stood unfired and with its ears missing on a low table. And there was a mysterious collection of telephones sitting in a silent but somehow expectant row along the mantlepiece.

She was cooking dinner when I got there—or rather, whipping up something in her blender with spinach and protein powder. It looked healthy, but disgusting.

"It's a new diet," she explained. "I made it up myself. I'm doing a purge. That's what I like about life," she added. "You can always start over."

I wasn't sure if she was referring to women with handcuffs or her digestive system, but didn't want to ask.

"You should have some. June said you went home sick."

"I'm not sick," I said. "But I do have a problem. You know that girl Trish who was at the shop the day before yesterday?"

I told her about Rosalie and the night at the strip, about Trish vanishing and my search for her.

"I don't know the slightest bit about the world she lives in, that's the trouble," I ended. "Not only am I not a teenager, but I don't know anything about prostitution."

Carole finished her drink, leaving a moustache of pale green above her lips. She licked it off thoughtfully. "I used to have fantasies about being a prostitute," she said. "I even turned a trick once."

"You?" I said, not sure if I'd heard her right. Carole was a little kooky, but it was hard to believe she'd gone to bed with a man for money.

She fixed me with her beatific, slightly vacant blue eyes. "Oh, it was no big deal — kind of strange, but not really upsetting. Funny, actually. . . See, I was taking an art class, well, really modeling for the art class in exchange for lessons. I was kind of into being naked — I mean, I was twenty or something and I had a good body and knew it. I really got into sitting up there, turning all different directions and stuff. I let myself fantasize, just in this general way. I wasn't a lesbian then, I guess I was bisexual, sort of pansexual, you know. I'd think about the women looking at me and at the men looking and it just felt good, it felt erotic."

She smiled warmly and almost playfully at me, and I realized I was trying to imagine what Carole looked like naked. She did have a nice body, especially wearing sweat clothes: lithe and energetic with just the right amount of curve at her thighs and breasts. If I were to admit it, at the moment she looked a little like one of those women in *Playboy* — guileless, a good sport, no hang-ups. I shook the image out of my head; it was too easy.

"So one day I'm leaving class and this guy comes up and asks if I want to go out afterwards and have a cup of coffee or something. He was just an ordinary guy, I can't even remember what he looked like. A little older than some of the rest maybe. 'Sure, why not,' I said, and we went to a coffee shop. Turned out he was married and had a couple of young kids. It wasn't like he was some sex fiend or anything. He didn't come on to me like that, just friendly and polite and asking me what I want to do for a living and how do I like the class and stuff. Then afterwards, when we're leaving the coffee shop, he all of a sudden asks, 'Your place or a motel?'

"'I don't think so,' I say, 'I mean, like you're married and everything,' I say, not to hurt his feelings. 'I mean, I like you and all, but . . .'

"'You don't understand,' he says. 'I want to pay you. It's just business. I'll pay you'—he says fifty dollars or something. It seemed like a fortune."

Carole seemed bemused at the memory. "Nowadays I'd tell him to get lost, *nowadays* something like that wouldn't even happen. But then . . . well, of course I needed the money, so some of it was that. But mainly I remember thinking, Wow, he thinks I'm a prostitute. Model equals prostitute, right? That was so—erotic! It gave me this great feeling, I don't know, like of being in control. Yeah, that's it," Carole repeated, twirling the blond lock of hair that fell out of her short hair like a question mark. "I felt powerful. And sexy, and sort of low and *nasty*."

I was speechless for a moment. "You *liked* that?"

"Umm-hmm," said Carole, smiling. "I did. It was sort of an extension of sitting up there on the platform, with my legs spread a little and thinking about being a sex goddess or something. They couldn't touch me, they were just sketching away, but I thought some of them would really like to. I could see it in their eyes."

I hastily lowered my own and asked, "So you went with him? How was it?"

"Oh, like most things," Carole said matter-of-factly. "Better in fantasy than in reality. We went to this creepy little motel and I took off my clothes and he took off his clothes and he did it, it only took about five minutes, and I didn't have much interest at all, I sure didn't get off or anything like that, and then we were both sort of embarrassed and didn't know what to say and he drove me home."

"And that was it?"

"Umm-hmm. I think it was mostly a fantasy thing for him too. He never really met my eyes or talked to me in class again."

She trailed off. We were sitting across from each other at the kitchen table and I was uncomfortably aware that I was doing a certain amount of fantasizing myself.

"I think a lot of women have ideas about being whores or strippers, don't you?" Carole said after a minute. "Wearing some depraved kind of costume, being powerful and in control, letting all that pent-up sexuality out. I mean, haven't you ever thought about it?" She regarded me innocently.

I searched my mind for pictures of me wearing a Frederick's of Hollywood black garter belt and push-up bra, but didn't find any.

"No, really," Carole pushed me. "What do you think of when I say the word 'whore.' 'Pam is a whore'?"

"I remember this time," I said slowly. "In junior high, ninth grade. Penny had just gotten a boyfriend, her first, and everything was different. Suddenly there was this pressure on me. I hadn't thought much about boys. I had this friend, Martha, and I was happy just spending time with her. But when Penny got a boyfriend, it was like I was supposed to have one too. That's the way it was with us. So I started going to parties, boy and girl parties. Finally I met someone's brother, a guy named Steve. He was two years older, sixteen, a junior in high school. I let him feel me up at the party. It was a little bit exciting, but mainly I was thinking, okay, now I have a boyfriend, now I'm going to be like Penny, now I'm going to be like everyone else.

"But Steve didn't call me after the party or ever again, and one night, very late, just as I was going to sleep, a carload of boys drove past the house. 'Pam is a whore!' somebody shouted. I looked out and it was Steve's car. I saw him.

"I was terrified, I was terribly humiliated, I didn't know what my parents would think."

"What did they think?" Carole asked.

"Oh god. My mother took me aside the next day for a little heart-to-heart talk. I tried to explain that I hadn't really done anything, and I think she believed me, but she went on and on about how boys could get the wrong impression, you had to be really careful how you acted. And so on. I felt like crawling under the bed and never coming out afterwards."

Carole took my hand and squeezed it sympathetically. Her touch was warm and lively and for a wild moment I thought of getting her undressed right then and there. Common sense held me back. Things didn't work that way. I should know that after this winter. If I slept with Carole I'd end up getting involved in her life, and that was the last thing I needed at this point.

Fantasy was better than reality, she'd said, and she was right. At least in this case.

I stood up. "I've got to get going. I'm on my way downtown to see if I can find Wayne."

She nodded, and I wasn't sure if she was disappointed or just feeling the effects of the spinach-protein drink. She looked a little sad. "I hope I didn't put you off. I mean, I'm a very sexual person, but I understand why you're upset about this girl being a prostitute and everything. It would be really strange to take your clothes off all the time and do it with hundreds of men."

"I don't think Trish feels it's very erotic," I agreed. "I'm not sure what she feels, but I don't think it has much to do with sex at all."

I drove away from Carole's feeling a mixture of relief that I hadn't done anything rash, and regret that caution had won out. It didn't suit me to be celibate and alone; I longed for the connection to my body that sex promised and often delivered. Why did the complications that being involved with real people who had pasts and expectations have to intrude? Why couldn't I—I stared at the garish signs of Lake City Way all around me and for the first time felt the persuasive logic of it all—just go out and find a prostitute?

16

$W_{\text{HEN I WAS A KID,}}$ Belltown was more often called the Denny Regrade, and that was what developers still called it. It was a strip along the bluff that had been bulldozed flat, between the city center and the foot of Queen Anne Hill, the traditional home of sailors and transients. Belltown was the old name, after William Bell, one of the city's first settlers, and that was still what the oldtimers and artists called it. It was one of those areas you never imagine becoming fashionable, but that do anyway. Martin Selig, Seattle's proverbial man with a million, who'd done more to change the city's skyline in five years than anyone else had managed to do in fifty, had put up large office buildings and condominiums along Third and Fourth. The streets next to the bluff, First and Second, were still hanging on, but soon the beat-up sailors' taverns, the hotels and odd little shops would be lost to the wrecking balls. In between the Sailors' Union of the Pacific and the Catholic Seaman's Club were whole blocks of two-story buildings boarded up and unoccupied, scheduled for demolition. The gentrification of the Market was creeping up First Ave. like a pretty disease, remodeling and refurbishing anything and everything into punk boutiques and European delicatessans.

It was strange to think that ten years ago you couldn't even get a croissant in this town.

The Redmond was a four-story brick apartment house built on one of the sloping streets between First and Western, in a no-man's land of vacant lots and withered blackberry bushes. There was a clump of men drinking Thunderbird out in front when I walked up to the door, but they let me pass without comment and with only a couple of leers.

The glass door had a star-shaped shatter near the knob and the lock was broken. I pushed it open and found myself in a filthy, dim hall illuminated by a single bulb. I saw a row of metal mailboxes, their little doors bent open, their locks forced, and found his name on one of them: W. Hemmings in an elaborate scrawl. 4A.

There was no elevator, of course, so I walked up, expecting at each turn of the stairs to find a nodding junkie or a rapist. By the time I reached the top I was a little winded. I was also wishing I had bothered to change my clothes again. The tweed jacket was fine if you were pretending to be a researcher, but it didn't provide much protection against the icy air that pervaded the building. We weren't far from Elliott Bay and you could smell the salt water in the draft.

His name was on his door and I heard some cheerful reggae music coming from inside. I knocked without having decided who I'd pretend to be for him, without, in fact, having any story prepared. It was going to depend on what he looked like, how he acted.

"Hi," he said when he opened the door, after having checked me out through the peephole.

"Hi," I said. "Look – ah, sorry to bother you, but I picked up a girl hitchhiking the other day and she told me this is where she might be reached. She, ah, left a book in my car and I wanted to return it to her. Her name's Trish."

I didn't know if this was at all believable. In fact, if Trish had talked to him on the phone yesterday he might know all about me – he might even have been expecting me.

But Wayne was a livelier and, on the surface at least, a less

73

suspicious character than his father, even though he looked something like him, with blond-red hair and a well-developed build. He was wearing a Hawaiian shirt and jeans, and had an open, sympathetic, tanned face.

"Sure," he said easily. "No problem. I'll give it to her when I see her."

I reached into my briefcase and slowly took out *Jane Eyre*.

"Listen," I said. "You mind if I talk to you a minute?"

There was no apparent hesitation.

"Sure, come on in. The place is kind of a mess, but I just got back from a trip."

The apartment did indeed look a mess, but it was a tasteful, well-heated one. It was a large studio with a loft in one corner and a curtainless view of the Sound and the enormous red neon "E" that hung over the Edgewater Inn. A large pine table by the window was strewn with brushes and paints and pads of paper. In another corner was a camera on a tripod facing a white screen, with a high stool in front of it. In the center of the room was a small red leather sofa and two matching chairs, arranged around a glass coffee table piled with art books and magazines. The stereo was a new and expensive one, with a number of record jackets stacked haphazardly around the speakers. There was a leather suitcase half-opened on the floor, with a few pieces of clothing still inside.

"Like a drink?"

"Just coffee."

He went off to a little kitchenette, moving to the reggae. I couldn't quite reconcile his reality with the picture I'd built up in my mind. Playboy maybe, but pimp and hustler? No, he couldn't be. He was too cute, too friendly, too good-humored. And obviously, he'd just come from a trip somewhere; no wonder Trish hadn't thought of calling him.

I stared at the suitcase; something about it bothered me, but I didn't know what. Some small thing seemed wrong.

I sat down on the sofa and looked at the art on the white walls. The paintings were pretty awful: large, lurid abstractions hinting at dog muzzles, fire hydrants, skyscrapers. The photographs weren't too bad: cityscapes with dramatic cloud formations and here and there a nude. I didn't recognize Trish's body.

"I haven't seen Trish for a while," he said conversationally, coming back with two cups of coffee and a can of condensed milk. "How's she doing these days?" he asked with warmth and apparent concern. I felt myself flush slightly. It had been some time since a man, especially one so much younger, had lavished such friendly attention on me, as if there was no question he found me attractive. It was disconcerting.

"She's a great kid," he continued, sipping his coffee. "Too bad there are so many family problems. I'm her stepbrother, I don't know if she told you..."

My nod could have been yes or no.

"...and I stayed with my dad and Melanie, his wife, and Trish, a couple of years back. I was sort of up in the air about what I wanted to do—whether I wanted to go to college or be an artist, you know. But Melanie developed some kind of thing against me. She really couldn't deal with my way of seeing the world. Definitely very threatening to the lady. I finally split just so there'd be some peace in the house between her and my dad."

I sipped my coffee. "Maybe she felt you were turning Trish against her?"

Wayne grinned self-deprecatingly. "Me? No, the lady just couldn't accept the fact that Trish was going through some changes, that she didn't think mama was the most wonderful person on earth anymore. My mother was the same way. But kids gotta grow up, right?"

"Was Trish hanging out with a bad crowd or something?"

"She was just doing what all kids do at that age—trying new things, meeting new people." Wayne raised a quizzical eyebrow. "I mean, didn't you? Come on, admit it," he teased. "You weren't always as sophisticated as you are now."

Me, sophisticated? He was having me on, but he knew it. There was a controlling quality underneath his boyish charm that was unnerving. If I were younger, if I were an adolescent, it might be attractive. Now I just felt annoyed and unsettled.

"Listen," said Wayne. "Trish was a smart kid and there was zero for her at that house. I mean, my father's a redneck, face it. A beer-guzzling, football-loving hick. My mother just married him to get away from home, to shock her parents. I mean, I like the guy and all, but I was raised pretty differently. My mother and I traveled, she made sure I was exposed to art and interesting people. I just wanted to share a little of the world's richness and variety with Trish. And old Melanie got jealous."

There was a knock at the door and Wayne excused himself to answer it. The man who came in seemed familiar somehow. Dressed in black chinos and a black leather jacket, he was in his early forties, bald, with sinewy arms, narrow shoulders and short, skinny legs. His black eyes were flat and unreadable as twin cameras with the lens caps on; he had a weak mouth and a silky black beard. The artist Trish had mentioned, one of Wayne's interesting friends.

"Karl Devize," Wayne introduced him, with a hesitancy I didn't expect. I didn't know if it came from respect or fear.

The name was familiar too. I'd read an article about Karl Devize in the newspaper a couple of years ago, when he'd first moved to Seattle. Something about bringing the East Village to Seattle and shaking up our provincial notions of art. "Misty skies and rain forests," Karl had scoffed when the reporter had asked uncertainly if he didn't admire at least *some* of the local artists. I'd been a little skeptical. Successful New York painters had better things to do with their time than shake the Northwest out of its dreamy dampness. Nor had the two reproductions of Karl's work impressed me much: flattened metal trash cans mounted on large canvases and spattered with dayglo paint.

"Pam Nilsen," I said. "I was just wondering if Wayne knew where to find a girl named Trish."

Karl grunted and sat down on the sofa. His hands shook slightly as he lit a cigarette. "Thought you were going to meet me at the Virginia Inn?" he said to Wayne. It had been better when he grunted; his voice was unpleasantly squeaky, as if there were a rubber mouse trapped in his larynx that the throat muscles kept stepping on. After his initial impassive look he hadn't given me a second glance.

"I don't suppose you've seen Trish?" I asked him.

He ignored me. "You just about ready, Wayne? I could use a drink." I had a feeling he'd already had several.

"Yeah, sure. I'm ready," said Wayne. He seemed flustered, as if he'd been caught doing something he shouldn't. He'd been acting the good-time party guy with an artistic streak for me, the concerned stepbrother who nevertheless hadn't seen Trish for ages. Now all he wanted was to get me out.

"I'm sorry I can't help you," he said. "I don't know what Trish has been up to lately. I've been gone a couple of weeks."

I thought he was emphasizing that a little too much, but I wasn't ready to challenge him on it. "I'm sorry too. If you see Trish tell her hi, though."

He showed me to the door, dancing a little to the reggae. Young, good-looking and devil-may-care, that was Wayne. I wondered how many paintings or photographs you had to sell to afford a set-up like this, how many girls you had to have working for you. Or were they working for Karl? Were they all—Wayne, Trish, Rosalie—working for Karl?

Before we parted he touched me on the arm with misplaced intimacy and gave me another one of his disarming boyish looks: Baby, we could be great together. No wonder Trish had been, was, bowled over by him.

"Be careful going down the stairs," he said softly. "This neighborhood's not the greatest."

"I think I can handle it."

"I'm sure you can, babe," Wayne said and smiled. "Come by anytime."

Just before the door closed I caught a glimpse of Karl staring at me from the sofa, his black eyes flat and hard.

17

I GOT INTO JUNE'S CAR and waited for a while, watching the door of the Redmond, but I didn't feel very cozy. It was true, as Wayne hadn't needed to remind me, that the neighborhood wasn't the greatest. Men alone and men in groups passed by me, not very purposeful and unsteady on their feet, but still menacing somehow. Nobody went in or out of the Redmond, and after fifteen minutes of freezing and feeling more and more vulnerable, I drove off to find a phone booth.

"June, it's Pam. Can you meet me at the Burger King on First and Pike in ten minutes?"

"I've already had dinner, thanks."

"It's not to eat. It's to help me shadow someone."

There was a pause of exasperation and then June said, "You are really taking this too far, girl."

"Come on, June, they'd recognize me. I need some reinforcements."

"*Some* people have children they just can't up and leave when the notion strikes them."

"Can't you take them to your mother's?"

"Somebody has my car last I knew. Besides, Eddy's here. We're having a nice quiet evening watching TV."

"That's even better," I said. "I'll pick you both up in five minutes."

I knew Eddy only slightly but I liked him. He was tall and quiet with a closely clipped Afro and glasses. He worked for City Light and I approved of him choosing June for company. She stirred him up and he calmed her down.

"I thought we were going to Burger King?" she said as I drove past it.

"No, I want you two to watch and see if this guy Wayne and his friend are in the Virginia Inn. Just go in there and have a drink and look for them. Wayne is kind of short, and good-looking and muscular, and he has reddish-blond hair and a tan, and he might be wearing a Hawaiian shirt. The other guy is bald with a black beard and a kind of blank mean look."

June and Eddy glanced at each other.

"Like I said, June," Eddy remarked. "Why stay at home watching *Miami Vice* when you can be living it here on the streets of Seattle?"

I dropped them off and parked the car. I spent an hour or so watching the activity on First and shivering, trying to put together what I'd learned today.

Everything that Beth, Melanie and even Rob had said had led me to believe that Trish was too dependent on Wayne for her own good. Which made her reluctance to see him after Rosalie's death pretty strange. According to Beth he was a manipulative pimp, with other girls, including Rosalie maybe, in his stable. Rob thought he was a nice kid, just a little spoiled by his mother, and Melanie loathed him. But even if he were a thoroughly corrupt character, what motive would he have for killing Rosalie and whisking Trish away? Assuming he lived off them, it wasn't likely he'd want to lose the income. He may have lied about not knowing where Trish was, but it didn't follow that he was a murderer. Whereas Karl looked like he could kill someone without blinking a matte black eye. If he had been the one to murder Rosalie he might have good reasons for wanting Trish away from the scene. Trish had said she was worried someone had seen her.

Was it Karl?

And then there was Rob. I didn't want to completely rule him out. There'd been so much venom in his red face when he'd talked about Trish. Male murderers were often obsessed with the sexuality of their victims, seeing them as depraved beings it was their duty to eradicate. And he had a bad temper and used to beat Trish, even though he'd denied it. And what had Melanie said? "He'd kill me if I got involved with Patti again." It was a long shot, but maybe he'd been following Trish, maybe he'd arranged to meet her to tell her something and Rosalie had gotten there first.

Maybe Rosalie wasn't the intended victim at all.

Finally June and Eddy came down the street and got into the car, a little tipsy and in very good spirits.

"Hey Pam, thanks for the nice evening. Too bad you couldn't join us," said June, pushing me into the passenger's seat. "Can we take you home? Looks like you could use a hot bath. Your teeth are chattering."

"Very funny. Well, did you see them?"

Eddy got in on the other side of me and attempted to bring my fingers back to life. "Hawaiian Shirt and Mr. Bald, yes indeed. Drinking tequila and having a great old time up at the bar."

"Were they with anybody?"

"Hard to tell. Your friends are popular guys, know a lot of people. They were already there when we came in, so we didn't see them walk in with anybody. They looked like they aimed to stay a while too."

"Sorry we couldn't stay longer," said June, starting the car. "Eddy and me, we got jobs to go to tomorrow, unlike some private investigators we know."

"Were there any women with them, any girls?"

"You mean Trish? Nope. Just a nice mix of professionals and regular old guys, everybody getting happily soused."

"Oh," I said.

"Particularly the bald guy. He had his own bottle, looked like."

"There was one thing, though," said Eddy. "At one point your friend Wayne said he wanted to make a toast: 'To a successful business deal.' Somebody who didn't seem to know him all that well asked if he'd sold a painting, and a lot of others laughed."

"You want my opinion, he's a dope dealer," said June on the way up to Capitol Hill. "And cocaine's the name of the game, the way he looks. Hawaiian shirts at the beginning of January. He obviously doesn't feel the cold—his snow is hot, not freezing."

I was less interested in linking Wayne and Karl to dope than to prostitution. In fact, all I really wanted to know was what they'd done with Trish and if one of them had killed Rosalie.

"I went and talked to Wayne earlier in the evening," I told June and Eddy. "He seemed so friendly and casual."

"That's the worst kind, honey," said June. "You never know where you are with them until it's too late."

18

I WENT BACK TO SEE BETH LINDA the next evening after work. The drop-in center was just as crowded as before; it was like fighting my way through a teenage party to get to her office.

"Well, you've certainly made the rounds," she said in her comforting deep voice, when she'd heard my stories of meeting Rob and Melanie, Wayne and Karl. "What do you think now?"

We were sitting in her tiny back office, surrounded by the bulging file cabinets and mountains of papers on the desk and chairs. Beth was wearing a turquoise and red tunic over black pants and a huge squash blossom necklace today. There was something both commanding and gentle about her presence, and it wasn't just her size. It was the sense you had looking at her, at her slightly weathered freckled face and calm green eyes, that (aside from the Carltons) she had learned to tame her devils.

"I guess I'd like to know more about what Trish has been doing for the past couple of years."

"I thought you might be back, so I got out Trish's files. I looked for something on Rosalie too, but either she never came in, or she used a different name. That happens pretty frequently." Beth put

82

on glasses and warned me, "This is confidential stuff, so I'm not going to let you read it; I'll just give you the main outline.

"She was first arrested over a year ago as a runaway. Loitering. The cops don't always pick up new kids for prostitution, especially if they've never seen them before. They give them what they call a talking to and what the kids call harassment and take them to the detention center where their parents or guardians pick them up. This happened twice with Trish — the detention center is a great place, by the way, to make new friends and learn the ropes. They bond with each other and the old hands teach the new ones.

"Okay, the third time, someone from the vice squad picked Trish up in a car and says she suggested an act of prostitution. That means money was mentioned. There's no way of knowing whether she suggested the act or the officer did. It's happened that a girl who's never done anything, who's just been hanging out on the street, will be approached by a man who offers her twenty bucks to go with him. She hasn't got any money so she says yes, and bam, she's in juvenile detention with a prostitute label on her that she'll never get off. Without having done anything. These are the kids we try to get to first with the outreach workers. Because once a girl has got that label, it's like a tattoo — it can't be washed off. The parents know, the cops know, sometimes the counselors and teachers at school know. She's officially a bad girl, a whore now — something that people can throw in her face anytime she steps out of line.

"And most of the time it becomes a self-fulfilling prophecy."

Beth looked somber and lit a Carlton. "I don't know exactly how it happened to Trish, but at any rate she became a chronic runaway. There were some meetings with her parents but they didn't go anywhere. You can see why. Her stepfather has it firmly fixed in his mind that she's a piece of trash, and her mom goes along with it. They signed her over to the state. The state placed her in a series of foster homes and she ran away from all of them. It's not surprising. The foster care system in Washington is a disgrace. A lot of people take in kids just for the money and there's no real way of checking up on them. Some of them abuse the kids, physically and/or sexually. The kids have no rights and no recourse, except to run. Other foster parents will take in a lot of different kids — so a kid from a relatively sheltered background will find herself in a house with drug addicts and shoplifters, kids who've never had a home, kids with a string of arrests, kids who can be abusive themselves.

"All this time it looks like Trish got little or no one-on-one counseling. She was in and out of school, failed the ninth grade, even though her test scores show that she's a bright girl with a high aptitude for English. It wasn't until she got institutionalized last spring that they found out she was on drugs, and that anyone seriously started to work with her. That's how it happens—and by then it's almost too late. A kid has such an internalized sense of degradation and hopelessness that it's hard to even get to her, much less get her out of the life. That's especially true of young prostitutes. Their sense of themselves as female has invariably been damaged. They're so distant from their bodies—they've had to become that way to survive—that they slip back into prostitution at the least opportunity. It's the easiest and for many the only way to make money. Especially if they use drugs.

"But Trish got some help and in some ways she was one of our success stories." Beth smiled briefly. "Not that we have overwhelmingly great standards for success. If a girl can get herself on birth control pills, that's a big step, and if she can remember to use a condom, that's another. Most of our girls have had VD and a lot of them have been pregnant. They know little or nothing about their bodies and their health is often really bad. I mean, you've seen them out on the streets in winter wearing practically nothing—and they don't eat right, Coke and french fries for days on end. We try to tell them about birth control and nutrition, but it doesn't usually sink in.

"Anyway Trish got placed in a halfway house about six months ago and started coming to weekly meetings for a group of young prostitutes, though, as I told you, she didn't always make it. But the group is good. It's a way for the girls to share some common experiences around pimps and customers and to get them talking about their feelings. Trish was also doing some school work here, working for her high school diploma.

"Then she ran again. It was in September and we lost sight of her. She wasn't picked up on the streets. I don't know if she stopped hooking for a while or if she was working through some massage parlor under a phony ID. But it was the last I heard of her until you turned up."

"You didn't go looking for her?"

"I tried. A little. But it's a big city and Trish is a smart girl, with an even smarter guy behind her. You don't get far with Wayne. And I've got my hands full with the kids who actually come here for help. I just figured – hoped – that Trish would pop up again."

"What do you know about a guy named Karl? A friend of Wayne's?"

Beth shook her head. "Trish never mentioned anyone besides Wayne." She looked tired. "I'm sorry I can't help you more, Pam, but my group for gay kids starts in ten minutes. I feel bad though . . . you know, you do care about each kid individually – but there are too many of them. Each with his or her own history and problems. You do what you can."

"I know," I said, and I felt the hopelessness of it.

19

PASSING BACK THROUGH the front room I saw the girl who had directed me to Beth in the first place, the paper-skinned teenager with the dyed black hair and glittering nose stud, who looked like she'd just dropped her teddy bear.

She was with another girl and studiously avoiding my eyes.

I went up to her anyway. "Hi," I said. "Remember me?"

Her companion looked me up and down, not unfriendly, just wary. She was probably all of thirteen, in a too-large Army jacket and black beret. "You work here?"

"No, but I'd like to talk to your friend a minute. What's your name?"

She made a helpless attempt to stare me down. It didn't work. "Cady," she murmured. She still had her cold. She waved her companion away.

"Thanks for telling me about Beth," I said. "I've talked to her and she's really been great. I'd just like to ask you two things — Do you know where Rosalie lived? And if so, will you take me there?"

"What makes you think I know anything?" Cady tugged

nervously at her black forelock and looked sideways at the video game players.

"Because you came up to me the other night. It makes me think you care about Trish and want to do something to help."

"Well, even if I knew, I couldn't do it now cause I got something to do here."

"Beth's group?"

She nodded. "And I'm late anyway."

"I'll wait for you then, over at the Clock restaurant. I can get you something to eat if you want and then you can show me."

I didn't think she'd go for it, but after a minute she sighed and agreed. It might have been the promise of food, though I liked to think it was because I was such a nice person.

I watched her go over to her friend and shrug. Then they both disappeared in back. I maneuvered my way through the crowd and walked two blocks to the all-night Clock restaurant.

I had a cup of coffee and thought about Carole. I found myself going through the same thought process I had all winter just before I slept with someone. The reasoning went something like this: First of all, Hadley was never going to come back to Seattle, admit it. I couldn't spend my whole life waiting around for her. Second, even if she came back to Seattle, what guarantee was there that she'd be interested in me? None. I mean, she'd been the one to break it off, right? Third, even if she *did* come back and *was* interested in starting up again, should I immediately fall into her arms and tell her yes?

Of course. I mean, of course not. She needed to be taught a lesson (even in absentia) and what better lesson to teach the girl of your dreams than that she was not the only game in town?

I let the waitress fill my cup again and grappled with a very simple reality: I wanted sex. And Carole promised sex and lots of it. Naturally June would be furious. Penny and Ray were couple enough in the collective and Carole was a dingbat besides (I could hear June already). But that was easy for June to say; she had Eddy. And I had no one. And no immediate prospects. Except Carole.

I put my head in my hands. Why had I thought that becoming a lesbian would solve all my problems? I'd thought that because last summer I'd fallen in love with Hadley and that *had* solved all my problems. At least temporarily. So why hadn't that damn woman stayed around? We could be having a Meaningful Relationship *right now*, and I wouldn't have had to go through all those stupid affairs to prove to myself that I was a lesbian. And to prove to my sister and everyone else that Hadley had been no mere flash in the pan. It was all her fault that I was even contemplating sleeping with Carole — an irrevocable act that I knew would bring me nothing but trouble.

Cady had the appetite of a horse — and she was as jumpy as one too. She gorged down steak and eggs and a piece of apple pie as well as two large Cokes, but the whole time she was looking around, at the waitresses, at the other customers and occasionally at me, as if she expected someone to come and snatch the food away from her any second.

I tried to put her at ease as much as possible, but her attention span seemed much shorter than Trish's, and she wasn't all that interested in the little I told her about myself, even when I mentioned I was a lesbian. I thought she might think we had something in common, but it was clear I just made her nervous. I was going to have to come up with a better life story if I was planning to hang around much with kids like these.

It wasn't until she'd finished her dessert that I brought up the subject of Wayne. "You know him?"

"Yeah," she answered briefly, warily. "He's cool."

"Is he Trish's old man?"

"*She'd* like to think so."

"But he's got other girls?"

"A couple."

"Are you one?"

"Me?" Cady looked upset. "I'm gay now. I don't go with no pimps. I've got better things to do with my money than give it to some dude." She slurped her Coke and blew her nose, a red lump with a glittering rhinestone in her soft, pallid face. "We were talking about pimps in our group. There's nobody who's ever had a good one."

"What about Karl — is he a pimp too?"

"I don't know him."

"Are you sure? Bald guy, with a black beard? An artist who's a friend of Wayne's."

Cady shook her head. "I don't hang out with Wayne, I don't know his friends."

"What about Rosalie?" I persisted. "Was she working for Wayne?"

"Maybe she used to," Cady said and put down her fork finally. "But she wanted to quit, she was trying to get off the street."

"You mean she wasn't working as a prostitute?"

"She stopped. When I saw her she said she didn't want to do it no more, she was sick of it. I know what she means."

"But Trish and Rosalie were staying together and Trish was working for Wayne. Did Trish want to stop too?"

"I guess," said Cady indifferently. "But probably Wayne wouldn't let her."

"You said Wayne was cool."

"Yeah, they're all cool, till they bust your head open. I had one guy when I was straight, he was more my boyfriend, another guy on the street my age. But it got to be a hassle, when I was making money and he was spending it. And I wasn't going to get pushed around by no dude who couldn't even support himself."

"Is Wayne different?"

"Wayne's got some class. I mean, he deals coke and shit so he doesn't have to live off girls or nothing. He's more like a friend. Like, he'd help you if you got in a jam, talk to people, get you a fake ID, loan you money..."

"And he doesn't ask anything in return?"

"Oh sure, you got to pay him back sometime...." She pushed away her plate and snuffled loudly into her napkin. "But you got to pay everybody back. He's no different."

Rosalie had lived in an old hotel in the city center, one of those pay-by-the-week fleabags. I guessed that Rosalie must have been paid up and that the desk clerk hadn't been reading the papers and didn't know she was dead, because he told us her room number without asking any questions and hardly a look at us. Since his job was not to see what was going on around him, that wasn't surprising.

"How are we going to get in?" Cady asked.

I'd read you could open doors with a credit card, but had never, before now, had occasion to try it. The lock was weak and my Sears card worked—another small side benefit of the market economy.

The room wasn't much to look at. There were the cactus plants on the sill and a few rock group posters tacked up on the wall. The double bed was neatly made and a Black rag doll, faded and once beloved, sat on the pillow. There was a small chest of drawers under a mirror; it had a large assortment of eye makeup and fingernail polish on it but not much else. The drawers were empty. Rosalie's—and perhaps Trish's—few clothes were hung in the closet or spilled out of a suitcase on the floor. The room had a stale, pathetic odor; two teenage girls, living on their own, one of them working as a prostitute, the other trying to stop. Had Trish supported Rosalie then? Or had Rosalie found other ways to make a living? Dealing dope, stealing? However they'd made their money, they hadn't ended up with much of it themselves.

Cady looked sad and uneasy. She picked up the Black doll and held it with unconscious longing. "What are you looking for, anyway?"

I shook my head. Maybe just a sense of Trish and Rosalie, a feeling for their life here. There certainly didn't seem to be anything to explain why Rosalie had died or why Trish was missing. Nevertheless I started looking through the clothes. There were T-shirts and underwear mostly, a few socks and stockings, a pair of Levis and a couple of sweaters. I went through the closet and found some fancier clothes: a red rayon dress, a kimono, a hanger full of cheap necklaces. Dress-up, play-acting clothes.

The last thing I did was take the blanket off the bed to reveal the faded, stained sheets, and run my hand between the mattress and box spring, where I hit something hard. I'd been looking for drugs; what I found was a diary with a broken lock. It was the padded, girlish kind that conjured up sweet secrets and emotional outpourings. I'd had one myself when I was thirteen—a yellow one for me, a blue one for Penny.

"I'll take this," I said, and put it into my bag. "I guess we can go now."

But before we left, I took one thing more: a tiny, silver-gray cactus in a ceramic pot. Cady kept the doll.

20

I FEEL LIKE KILLING MYSELF," the diary began. It was in November, over two years ago, when Trish was thirteen, in the eighth grade. "I don't have any friends. Yvonne was my friend but she moved away. All my teachers except Mrs. Smith hate me, she said I wrote a good paper for English. It was about Nagasaki, a book I read. It made me feel so bad to know what we did in the war to the Japanese. I hate people, especially Rob. Now he has been married to Mom six months. At first he pretended to be nice, he said he would teach me to play softball, but then he said I was getting too old. I guess Mom told him I got my period. I hate my Mom how she is around him. She and I used to get along and talk and everything. Now he's here every night the fat slob, he sits watching TV and doesn't say anything. If I get a bad grade he yells at me. Yesterday he said something mean about my boobs, I can't help it if they're getting big. My Mom never says anything. I hate her. I feel like killing myself."

Outside my apartment the night was quiet and cold. I was drinking tea under the quilt but I was still cold. Ernesto maintained an injured distance on the rocking chair.

"December 10. Rob hit me last night, it was the first time he hit me so hard. I forgot to take out the trash this morning and so the trash collectors didn't pick it up. Big fucking deal. My Mom started crying but she didn't do anything. She just said Patti why can't you do what you're supposed to do so Rob doesn't have to get angry. Then she said why can't you be like you were before. She should know. I'm the same as I always was. It's him that's the problem.

"I told Heather about it in PE today. She said her Dad hits her too and once he gave her a black eye. She asked if I wanted to eat lunch with her and her friends. Heather is cool, she has a lot of friends and a boyfriend Sam, he's in high school and he has a motorcycle."

"December 26. I gave Heather a necklace and she gave me a stuffed bear. We went to the park and Sam came over and gave us a ride on the motorcycle. He said he would introduce me to his friend. He gave us some pot. Heather said she smoked it all the time, so I said I did too, but I never tried it before. Her parents were gone so we went back to Heather's house and got high. First I didn't feel anything then I felt dizzy. I pretended I liked it though. We made brownies because we were hungry. I came home late and Rob slapped me."

The first entries were in a large, well-formed script that got smaller and more sloping as it went on, as if that could help minimize the events. I followed Trish through the eighth grade, through Rob's beatings and her increasing lack of feeling about them. She seemed to take them for granted and only reported them when they were especially bad, like the time he raised welts on her back. Her grades dropped and she got high more often. Heather's boyfriend disappeared from the picture, but then the two girls met Jamie and Mark, two boys in the ninth grade, and hung out with them. So far it was a childish diary that was not so different in many ways from what I wrote at her age. In spite of being filled with thoughts about the stupidity of her family and of school, it was unselfconscious and gave no hint of what was to come.

Then, that summer, Wayne arrived to stay with them.

"*June 20*. Wayne and I spent all day talking today while Rob and Mom were at work. He speaks Spanish and has traveled all over the place. He said they tested him when he was a kid and they found out he had an IQ of 180 so his Mom didn't care if he went to school or not. He's read everything. I never talked to anybody about books before outside of school. He asked me what I was reading and I told him I was reading *David Copperfield*. We had to read part of that in school and I wanted to finish it. He said he was reading Frowd and Young when he was my age. He said he'd been psychoanalyzed (I looked that word up, also it's Freud and Jung), and you can tell a lot about yourself from your dreams. They have symbols. A lot of the symbols mean something about your sex life. A woman is a circle and a man is a stick. So if you dream you're playing ping-pong with someone, the shape of the paddle means you're having intercourse with them. I didn't know that."

"*June 26*. Wayne gave me some books to read. One is named *Fanny Hill*. It's about a fifteen year old girl in the 18th century who turns into a whore and it's a classic. It's written in old-fashioned language that's hard to understand. So far it's sad because Fanny is an orphan and has to sell herself to make money. Wayne doesn't have a girlfriend. He used to but she got boring. She wanted to have sex all the time, she was a nimfomaniac. Wayne said he had sex the first time when he was thirteen with one of his mother's friends. She was an artist and she was married but her husband didn't care. He used to watch them. I said that was disgusting. Wayne said it was funny. He said it should be like that, somebody should teach you. He said he likes to have a lot of girlfriends because then you don't get tired of sex because everybody is different. Freud is one who talks about sex. Jung is more about mythology. Wayne took me to a photographic exhibit of nudes. He said people should love their bodies. I hate mine, my boobs are too big. Wayne said I'd grow into them."

*

"*June 28*. Heather called and wanted me to go swimming and then to the mall to meet Jamie and Mark. But I said I didn't want to. I think Heather is really stupid, she never reads anything and the only thing you can discuss with her is boys. Wayne and Rob got into a fight tonight. Rob said he should be looking for a job. Wayne said he just got to Seattle and he didn't know his way around yet. I thought Rob would hit him but he didn't. They watched a baseball game on TV and drank beer. My Mom was upset about something, she went in her room. I think it's better when Wayne is here, then Rob doesn't hit me. I am reading *Fanny Hill*. Wayne came in to say good-night and I was reading it. He said my nightgown was sexy. I wanted him to kiss me but he didn't. I love him so much. I can't think of anything else."

"*July 1*. I told Heather I was in love with Wayne and she said it was incest. But it's not because he's not my family. She asked if we did 'it.' We talked about sex, she used to do it with Sam. If you do it standing up you don't get pregnant. I asked Wayne but he said it wasn't true. He said it was too bad there wasn't more sex education. He asked me if I ever masturbated. I said I did when I read some parts of *Fanny Hill*. Then I was really embarrassed!"

"*July 2*. I went swimming with Heather. When I came back home I didn't think anybody was here. Then I heard Wayne in Rob and Mom's room, he called to me to come in. The curtains were closed and he had a lamp on. He was reading one of Rob's *Playboy* magazines and he was rubbing himself. He asked me if I had ever seen a man's penis before. I said no, but I guess I saw my Dad's a couple times. He asked me to rub him up and down. It seemed weird because he had never even kissed me but I did it because I love him. After a while the white stuff came out and he got soft again and talked about books and things. He asked me if *Fanny Hill* had given me any ideas. I said there were a lot of things I didn't understand, but he said he would explain them. The main thing to remember he said is that sex is fun and people should do it as often as they can. At the end he kissed me. I love him to kiss me."

"*July 6*. Wayne says he won't hurt me. Every day except the Fourth of July I rub him. It's kind of boring except when he kisses me. He showed me the pictures in *Playboy* and explained the jokes. He said the girls have hair down there but they brushed it out for the pictures. He asked if he could see me down there but I felt stupid because I didn't look like those girls. Then he asked me to suck him. First it grosses you out but I guess it's the same as rubbing. It's weird to see Wayne get so excited but then he says, Baby I love you and kisses me. I hate the taste though."

"*July 8*. Today we went to a guy Wayne just met named Karl who's an artist, and smoked some pot, then he gave Wayne some pills. I was bored, I went to the bathroom, when I came back out I heard Karl say, can I have some when you're through and Wayne laughed and laughed. Wayne says he knows a lot of people who use coke. It's the best drug but it's expensive. He's going to get some from Karl."

"*July 9*. Today we did 'it.' I knew it would hurt because it hurt Fanny Hill the first time, but not that it would hurt so much. I guess I liked it. I like to be close to Wayne. I feel like he's always going to take care of me and watch to make sure nothing bad happens."

21

THERE WAS A BREAK AFTER THAT and when the diary started again it was as if a different Trish were writing, jaded and cynical. She was cutting classes regularly in the ninth grade. She hated all her teachers except Mrs. Horowitz in English. She didn't have many friends and she didn't seem to feel too well physically. There were a lot of references to "being out of it" all day, to oversleeping and having her mother yell at her. Some entries seemed to be written under the influence of drugs. They were full of strange thought associations, visions and an obsession with death. She no longer talked of killing herself, but of being close to some self-destructive edge that attracted as much as frightened her.

Wayne was still living at home, but seemed to be increasingly gone from the house. There were a lot of references to "looking for W.," "W. at K.'s house," "W. says he needs to see K." Was K. Karl or another girl? Trish seemed jealous and miserable. She no longer mentioned kissing, but sometimes went on for paragraphs about how she loved W., dwelling on his hair, his eyes, his voice.

Then, in November, Rob kicked Wayne out of the house. There was a big blow-up and the beatings began again. The difference now was that Trish didn't passively accept it, but fought back. And she started running away. To W.'s usually. But sometimes W. wasn't around. He was at K.'s and then at N.'s. Trish ended up downtown looking for him.

New initials began to make their appearance and the entries became more and more cryptic. It appeared that Trish was making dates or keeping appointments.

On January 15, a year ago, she wrote, "Went to K's. Two guys in exchange for a gram. W. happy. Bought me dinner and told me I should get out of Rob's for good. Could make a lot of money, get new clothes. Offered to set me up. I don't know. When I'm high I feel like I could do anything, it doesn't touch me, but the next day I hate myself. Last week a guy at the clinic told me I had gonorrhea and gave me penicillin. I didn't tell W. He's not going to catch it from me until he gives up S."

A few days later she was in the detention center, picked up for prostitution. She got out the next morning but wrote, "Rob called me a whore. Mom just cried. I didn't care, I felt like a whore, I really did. I didn't before I was arrested, I was pretending it was something else. Now I'm not. I never want to go back to school again. I hate them all. I hate Wayne. I'm not going to see him anymore. I'm just going to stay here in my room and rot."

But she didn't. She ran away again. Was picked up again. And again. Suddenly she was in a foster home.

"*March 4*. The lady who's my foster mom says she doesn't care what I do as long as I come home by eleven. She also said no drugs in the house but she wouldn't know if I was high, she's drunk half the time anyway. Yesterday she told me her life story when she was drunk. She got pregnant when she was seventeen and had to leave high school, her first husband ran off with another woman and her second husband just ran off. She has three kids, the oldest one is eleven and already has a record for shoplifting. She doesn't work and makes her money from foster kids. She told me if I wasn't careful I'd end up like her. Fat chance. I'd kill myself first."

*

By the following month Trish was in another foster home where they would hardly let her out of their sight. She ran away from them to W.'s who turned her on to some really good speed. It sounded like she was shooting it.

The diary stopped and didn't take up again until late summer and again it was a different Trish writing, a little older and wiser. She'd been through a drug abuse program and was clean. She was living at a halfway house and attending a group for prostitutes. There were few references to Wayne and they were all in the past tense, but a lot about Beth Linda and some of the girls in the group.

"*August 5*. Julianne started crying in the group tonight, talking about how her Dad started having sex with her when she was only six. She didn't understand what was going on until she was older and by then it seemed too late to tell her Mom, because she'd say Julianne had been doing it for too many years. Julianne started running away when she was eleven. A lot of these girls seem really stupid to me and I don't think Julianne can even read. But then I think, I've been stupid too, even though I thought I was acting so grown-up and reading all those books Wayne gave me. Then Julianne said something that really shocked me, she said she didn't feel anything in her body anymore and she thought it was because when she was little she would just pretend it wasn't happening to her, like she would just close it all off. And that was weird because I know that feeling. So many times I was high and I didn't think about what I was doing. Sometimes I couldn't even remember what I'd done, it was like a bad dream. A couple of other girls in the group said that too. It was weird to think you can stop feeling like that.

"Beth said it happens a lot. That it's a way of protecting yourself. She said to think about how you maybe did it not because you hated yourself and hated to think about what you were doing, but because deep inside you loved yourself and that was the only way you could protect yourself. She said a lot of girls get things done to them by people who say they love them. It's like a mixed message and it screws up your trust for people. She said we shouldn't think of ourselves as victims but as survivors. We were all alive and we were here to change some bad parts about our lives and get more in control.

"It was a good meeting, but afterwards I felt depressed. I thought about how happy I was last summer when I first met Wayne, and thought I was learning so much about the world. It was like we had a real friendship and he was teaching me about psychology and literature and everything. He said he loved me but he just let me get all screwed up. It's weird that he's never gotten hooked himself. Maybe if you're a dealer you don't. I guess it was my fault though. I guess that's why he got tired of me."

"*August 12.* I told Beth I had read some Freud and Jung. She said she liked Jung better because he was more hopeful. We talked about dreams and she asked me if I ever wrote mine down. I said it was hard to remember them, but she said if you thought about it you could do it. She said she'd done that once and it had helped her. She told me that she'd been an alcoholic and that she'd had a baby when she was fifteen. She wasn't like that foster mother who said to watch out, I'd end up like her. Beth said you can change, you can do anything you want to."

"*August 19.* In the group tonight Julianne said she went to her father and told him what he'd done to her. She said it had been hard but it had made her feel a whole lot better. Beth called that confrontation. She said it could be dangerous, but that it could also make you feel more in control and assertive. She said a lot of times the man would lie and say he didn't do anything and you just had to expect that. Julianne said her father told her she was crazy and didn't say he was sorry at all, but *she* knew. This made me start remembering a lot of things I didn't think I remembered. I thought about confronting Wayne. I don't know what I would say. First I loved him and then I hated him, but somewhere inside I still love him. I haven't seen him for almost three months.

"Last night I dreamed that he and I were sailing in a boat. It was on a lake with the sun setting. He was reading a book to me. At first it was a fairy tale kind of thing with a princess and a king. He started explaining it all to me though and it got dirtier and dirtier. Pretty soon it was just words like fuck and dick and cunt coming out of his mouth. I put my hands over my ears so I couldn't hear him. And then all of a sudden it was nice again. He looked so handsome and sweet, smiling at me with his lips moving, but with no words coming out to spoil it."

And then, abruptly, the diary ended. The last couple of pages had some notes and addresses, including one for Art Margolin in Portland. Her father. She must have bought another diary, perhaps she had it with her now, wherever she was. Perhaps it told about confronting Wayne and falling in love with him again, about dropping the group and taking up prostitution again, about Rosalie and what had happened to her.

It was two when I fell asleep and my dreams were sad, violent ones.

22

Iᴛ ᴡᴀsɴ'ᴛ ᴇᴀsʏ to get the blood out of the back seat. June came over early the next morning and we took a pail of soapy water and a bottle of all-purpose spray cleaner down to the car along with rags and a stiff brush.

"This is something you never see on TV," June commented. "Bang, bang, and then a commercial. If Magnum, P.I. had to clean up after himself you'd see a whole different type of show. Hey, he could even do his own commercials – 'If *you* have trouble getting out those stubborn blood stains after a big shoot-up, try FLEX. And *see* the difference!'"

I needed her humor, especially after reading Trish's diary last night. I told her about it and about going to Rosalie's old hotel room.

"I was hoping the diary would give me some clue about who killed Rosalie and why Trish disappeared, but it ended last fall, with an entry about confrontation. I suppose Trish went to Wayne to confront him and that's how she got involved with him again. But the diary doesn't have much about Karl and nothing about Rosalie."

"You ever think that old Trish herself killed Rosalie, used you to make her getaway and to screen her from the cops, and then went into hiding on her own?"

"You know that can't be true, June," I said, scrubbing with an averted face. "If you'd seen her that night. She was so upset... No, I keep thinking about what Cady said, that Rosalie wanted to get out of prostitution. If she was working for Karl or Wayne maybe that's why they killed her. Or maybe she was involved with them in some kind of drug ring, and tried to rip either one or both of them off. She had to make money *some* way if she wasn't hooking."

"And Trish was seen by the murderer and had to keep low?" June was inside the car now, trying to get into the corners of the backseat.

"Especially if it was Karl or Wayne," I said. "Especially if she thought she might have been the one they were trying to kill."

"Tell me about this Karl character."

"There's not a whole lot to tell. Cady said she didn't know him or if he was a pimp or not, and there are only initials in Trish's diary for the most part. She only mentioned him directly once, when Wayne met him. But you should have seen Wayne when Karl came into the room. Wayne was nervous, like a little kid trying to please him almost. What if he was totally under Karl's influence, what if Wayne was just a mock pimp, a front man for Karl? What then?"

June muttered something indistinct and I went on. "That still doesn't solve the problem of where Trish is, and if she's in danger. She could be hiding on her own, or Wayne could be hiding her from Karl or Karl could be hiding her from Wayne."

June climbed out of the Volvo. "I don't suppose it's occurred to you that Trish might have just wanted to get away from *you*? Maybe she didn't like mothering all that much. Maybe she was afraid you'd turn her in after all."

"Maybe," I admitted, though that hurt a little. "But she wrote me that note, June. She said she'd be back." I wrung out my cloth and tried to think. "Or what if it was her stepfather who killed Rosalie, I mean, what about that possibility? Would Trish try to tell her mother, or would she want to keep it a secret? Even though she hates him, maybe she'd want to protect her mother."

"Aren't you forgetting about the Green River killer? It could have been a total stranger who got Rosalie."

"The Green River killer is probably long gone by now – they just keep finding bones two and three years old and no traces of the guy. He could have moved to another state, anything. Just because a girl gets killed doesn't mean it was him."

"That's right. Girls get killed every day. No big deal. But did you ever think of the possibility that one of those guys, Rob, Wayne or Karl *is* the Green River killer? I mean, take Wayne. . ."

"That's impossible," I said shortly. "It's hard for me to think that someone like Wayne killed one woman, much less forty or seventy or however many it is. He may be a pimp and drug dealer, but I can't believe he's a serial murderer. He's too smooth."

"That's exactly the type," said June, stepping back and scrutinizing her labors. "Look at Ted Bundy, Republican campaign worker, law student, good-looking charm boy, going around with his arm in a sling to ask college girls, 'Excuse me, dear, but I'm temporarily incapacitated. Could you please open my car door for me. . .'" June approached me with an ingratiating grin. "And then, bop! They still can't lay a count to all those girls – Washington, Utah, Colorado, Florida. There was a raving maniac behind that handsome face. Or what about that guy they called the I-5 Killer, the star athlete, who almost had his picture in *Playgirl*? Cruising up and down the Interstate looking for women working in out-of-the-way Burger Kings. 'A large Coke and french fries, honey, and while you're at it, into the back room so's I can rape and murder you.' He killed over forty girls. And nobody could believe it. 'My little baby,' his mom said. And he had a fiancée who was head over heels about him too. Those are the guys to watch. Finished? Let's go in and get some coffee."

"Why are all the serial killers in Washington?"

"'Cause it's roomy and wild out here. And we've got all these cool highways. You don't get girls into your car in New York City – you gotta kill 'em on the subway and then people see you. Plus, it's a lot easier to get a gun permit in the West. You know, I was reading statistics in some magazine. Over ten thousand deaths from handguns in the U.S. last year. In the rest of the world it was like forty to fifty a year and in England it was only eight. Who says the frontier days are gone? Shoot 'em up, baby!"

"Yeah, but Ted Bundy strangled his victims and Rosalie was knocked out with a crowbar or something."

We both looked at the pink-dyed water in the bucket. June dropped her joking tone.

"Maybe you ought to call the police and tell 'em what you know. Maybe they've got something on one of those guys already."

"I would—if I knew more, and if I knew where Trish was. Anyway the police won't be impressed by my suspicions. I've got to find out more. I just hope I'm not too late. . ." I stopped and looked at June. We were both thinking the same thing.

It was a beautiful cold clear day at the airfield in Issaquah. The women's skydiving club was assembled and ready to go, parachutes, helmets and boots on.

"Can't I just watch you from the ground?" I asked. "I think I'd like that perspective better."

"Nobody's going to push you out," June assured me from somewhere inside her helmet. Her brown eyes sparkled. "Don't worry, you'll love it. The view's spectacular. We're really lucky with the weather. You'll be able to see Mount Rainier."

The plane was tinier than I'd imagined. I sat next to the pilot, a taciturn fellow named Alvin with a pustular red face. I hated to think he might be the last thing I saw before we went down.

We shot up at a forty-five degree angle that brought my stomach level with my eyebrows. I didn't know how June expected me to see anything. In order to keep breathing I had to keep my eyes closed. The noise was deafening. Finally we straightened out and I risked a peek. It was spectacular all right. Lake Sammamish on one side, the sharp, sparkling white Cascades on the other, and to the south, the massive snow cone of Mount Rainier, looking like something out of Hiroshige.

"Ya ready, gals?" Alvin called back to June and the others, after he had circled up over the airfield a few times.

"Yeah." They got ready and then one of them (in their bulky jump suits it was difficult to see who) moved to the open door.

Penny had told me she had a safe feeling when she jumped, as if she were being cradled in the wind. I found that impossible to believe. How could anyone feel safe at 10,000 feet? I didn't feel safe climbing a ladder. And certainly not sitting in the cockpit of this rickety little plane.

Far below us I saw the bright spread of the parachute drifting like a candy wrapper in the breeze. Two insect legs kicked out, and then she was on the ground, no more than two minutes after she'd jumped. All this fuss for a hundred seconds of weightless fear?

One after another they jumped and drifted. Alvin hummed a tuneless little tune, and then he brought us down to safety with a bump.

"Isn't it great, Pam?" June enthused, gathering up the folds of her parachute. "What a feeling! There's nothing like it."

My legs shook as I walked away from the airplane and towards her. "Yeah, great," I said weakly.

"We're going up again, want to come?"

"I'd love to, but — I just remembered something important I have to do."

"What's that?"

"Stay alive."

When I got home there was a message from Carole on my machine.

"Hi, uh, hi Pam. Uh, this is Carole. Hi!" She was speaking in the loud, awkward voice people use when they are being tape-recorded with nothing much to say. "Well, I, uh, was wondering. Well, give me a call, okay? This is two p.m., Saturday," she hastily added and hung up.

Her normal voice, when I called her back, was warm and lively as usual. She wanted to go to a midnight movie, and, when I expressed some hesitancy about being able to stay awake that long, she described it in such bizarre detail that I began to feel I'd already seen it, or at least Carole's vision of it, culled from obscure reviews in years past and various hearsay reports.

"It's the kind of thing that really gets you thinking, like about past lives and the Apocalypse and brain cannibalism and stuff. . ."

"What if we got together earlier?" I suggested, uneagerly. All I really wanted was to go to bed with her, not to become her friend, and as a good feminist, that made me feel guilty. On the other hand, maybe that was all she wanted too. Perhaps by some miracle we could have sex and never speak of it afterwards. . .

not very likely... vivid pictures rose up before me of dramatic tearful scenes in the darkroom, of June's disgusted face, of Penny and Ray coming home to find another messy collective split. "Maybe we could just go out for dinner, make an early night of it ...I'm pretty tired..."

"Oh, I'd love to come over and go out," Carole said enthusiastically. "I'll be by about seven, all right?"

"All right," I agreed, wishing there was a pill you could take to induce willpower and caution, and knowing that even if there was, I might not want to swallow it.

23

As soon as I hung up I started going through the Yellow Pages calling the art galleries. Most of them claimed never to have heard of Karl Devize, or said they thought he'd gone back to New York, but the smallest and nastiest of them said they did have some of his work and asked me hopefully if I were an interested buyer.

"I'm actually trying to get his studio address," I admitted. "It's kind of a...family emergency."

I wondered if real detectives had to lie so much, or if they did it so badly. But perhaps my amateurishness stood me in good stead. Even to myself I sounded like a slightly breathless relative. And I got the address.

Karl's studio was at the far end of Belltown, in an old industrial building by the water. It was twilight by the time I got there and a Dickensian salt fog enveloped the waterfront. The dampness crept inside my down parka and into my bones and it was hard to remember that only a few hours ago I'd been up in an almost cloudless blue sky, looking over at Lake Sammamish and the Cascades. Peering into the murky hallway that led to Karl's studio I wasn't sure which was worse—sun and vertigo, or gloom and my feet on the ground. I felt frightened of Karl somehow, and far less sure of my ability to handle him compared to Wayne.

I found his door and knocked, waited and knocked again. I tried the knob and discovered it was unlocked; I was wondering whether to walk in when I heard Karl's unmistakable squeaky voice call out, "Come in, man, come in."

The studio was small and dark and smelled of garbage and cat shit. The windows facing the Sound had been covered with tar paper and the only light came from a couple of table lamps without shades sitting on the floor. They cast small, harsh lights around their perimeters and dimly illuminated the extraordinary array of junk packed into the room. Bed springs and old pipes, car parts, an old wood stove, television sets and radios with their wires sticking out, everything metallic and greasy you could imagine.

In the middle of this second-hand shop sat Karl in an armchair. He had a white cat on his lap and a bottle of tequila in his hand. From his sunken posture and glazed black eyes it seemed he was well on the way to drunkenness. He didn't seem to recognize me at all.

I immediately decided to drop any pretense of being there to take a look at his art. I might have been mistaken, but from what I could see there didn't seem to be any around.

"I met you the other night at Wayne's," I said. "I'm still looking for Trish Margolin. I know you know her."

Karl's bald head dipped and he stroked the white cat. He didn't seem surprised that I was there; maybe he was used to women, real or ghostly, popping up in his amateur junk shop to confront him.

"She's a nice girl, Trish," he finally said, placatingly, in his rubber mouse voice that the tequila made even shriller. "They're both of them nice kids, great kids."

This wasn't what I'd expected at all.

"Do you know where she is?" I moved towards him a little and stumbled over a piece of pipe. It made me think of Rosalie and how Miranda had said she'd been bludgeoned by a heavy instrument.

"You'll have to ask Wayne," Karl said, peering at me. There was a delayed gleam of recognition in his eyes. "You were over at his place the other week, weren't you?" Instead of making him suspicious, this realization seemed to reassure him and make him more confiding. "Wayne knows, he always knows where Trish is. Weeks can go by, months, Wayne always knows where she is, helps her, takes care of her no matter what trouble she's in. She's his girl, his sister you know, sort of. She's always been his girl, right from when I first moved to Seattle." Karl looked befuddled as he tried to remember when that might have been, and drank a little more to clear his head. "I thought he had promise, not like some of them in this city. Took him under my wing, taught him everything I know, introduced him to people, helped him get started. . . ." Karl gestured around to his packed studio as if that explained everything. "I came here to kick the art scene in the balls. And I did, I sure as hell made them think again."

He'd probably put the tar paper over the windows then—to make sure he wasn't influenced by the misty sky and sea.

I took a breath, trying not to smell the garbage, and asked, "Did you know that Trish was working for Wayne?" I was counting on the fact that Karl was too drunk to wonder why I was asking and hoping that he wouldn't remember enough of the conversation to repeat it to Wayne.

"Sex is a beautiful thing," squeaked Karl, and stroked the white cat. "A young girl, a young man . . . We're not all young, though," he added gloomily. "You don't make money as an artist, not if you're any good. Now in New York, I sold my paintings for thousands of dollars—I would have sold them anyway, if I'd wanted to sell them, if I thought people deserved to have them. But Seattle is too tight-assed to appreciate the avant-garde. It's a Boeing Corporation town and what the Boeing directors say is art, everyone thinks is art. The phoney-baloney symphony they're so proud of, the fucking Pacific Northwest Ballet, and the paintings they can hang on the walls of their boardrooms. Mountains," he mumbled in conclusion, "everyone wants fucking mountains. I say piss on mountains."

"So Wayne needed money and got Trish to work for him."

"You're too uptight, lady," said Karl regretfully, lifting the bottle to his lips. A trickle wet his silky black beard. "You must be from Seattle. You see things in black and white. There's nothing wrong with sex. It didn't bother Trish."

"And Rosalie and the others too?"

"Rosalie?" he sounded bewildered. "There was Abby for a while, but she was a real bitch. Not like Trish. Trish was always Wayne's girl, she'd do anything for him. It was beautiful."

"What happened when Trish went away last year? What did you and Wayne live on then?"

"Drugs!" Karl gave a rubbery whinny and the white cat yawned. "We lived on drugs and tequila. Girls are just the...the frosting on the cake."

"So Wayne is a dealer."

"Hey." Karl looked like he was on the edge of a suspicion for the first time. "Why are you asking me all these questions?"

"I'm not asking...," I said hastily. "I'm just looking for Trish. Want to tell her something."

"Oh...." He seemed mollified, or at least he subsided back into his alcoholic stupor. "I taught Wayne everything he knows," he said again. "I was like a father to him. Coke, speed, I got him connections. Like a goddamned father...." Karl rambled down and resumed petting his cat.

I started to wonder if it was all an act. Wayne's obvious nervousness, his need to get me out when Karl came into his studio the other day—what had that meant? Karl must know more about Trish and Rosalie than he was letting on. I tried one last question, a wild guess.

"Did Wayne have a good time in Hawaii?"

"Hawaii? What was he doing in Hawaii, he wasn't in Hawaii, was he?" Karl stared at me. "He said he was just going to Portland overnight. But you tell me he was in Hawaii, that little cocksucker." Karl's flat black eyes grew moist. "I've never been to Hawaii. That's the way, you teach them all you know and then they fucking go to Hawaii. They cut the ground out from under your feet, fucking ungrateful bastards."

I couldn't get any more out of him after that, and I didn't even feel like trying. The fumes of the garbage and cat shit were starting to get to me, and when I finally stood outside his door, I breathed in long gasps of fresh air.

But who the hell was Abby?

24

I STILL HAD HALF AN HOUR before Carole and I were to meet. I raced home and called June. "Just wanted to make sure you landed all right," I said. Then I asked her if she knew what cocaine was selling for these days.

"Pam, you just got back on the ground. Why don't you stay here?"

"No, I'm serious. I need to see Wayne again without him thinking I'm looking for Trish."

"But Pam, you haven't watched enough TV to know how to do a drug deal."

I had once asked June why she watched so *much* TV. She'd said it was because there were so many Black actors these days. "I see more Black people on television than I see in downtown Seattle. Every cop show has at least one—hey, sometimes they're even the co-star, imagine that!"

Now it turned out that TV might be instructive in other ways, too.

"You'll just have to explain it to me," I said.

*

111

"I can't figure Karl out," I told Carole when she arrived, bubbly and a little too cleverly dressed in red stretch pants and a hand-painted linen jacket with enormous padded shoulders. "I'd been imagining he was behind the whole thing, the malevolent kingpin who directed Wayne and Trish to his own evil ends. Now I wonder if he's not just a drunken failure holding on to Wayne for dear life. But then, why would Wayne have acted afraid of him?"

"Maybe because Karl knows something. He might not have done anything, but maybe he *knows* something," Carole said. She bounced around my apartment looking at things.

I dismissed this. "I think I got out of him everything he knows. Sex is beautiful, he said, when I was trying to talk to him about Wayne pimping Trish. A young man, a young girl. Pah! Young girls and disgusting old men is more like it."

"Sex *is* beautiful, Pam." Carole stopped her investigation of my record collection and fixed me with an earnest look. "Don't you think so?"

I thought she was hopeless, but that didn't stop a small rocket from shooting up through one thigh and into my solar plexus. "What do you know about coke, Carole? Ever buy any?"

"Wow, Pam," she said, and her blond hair stood up, perky, thrilled. "You're much more exciting than I ever imagined."

I thought about giving Wayne a call before we turned up, but didn't want to give him the advantage of expecting us. It was going to be hard enough to find out what I wanted to know.

I drove down to Belltown, carrying on a halfhearted conversation with Carole about drugs. I said that marijuana made me sleepy and coke destroyed the economies of Third World countries so I never touched it, and the last time I'd tried a hallucinogen I'd seen my face staring at me from under Penny's haircut, so I'd given that up too. Carole said she was just naturally high and she only used drugs as aphrodisiacs.

Is it any wonder I had ideas?

We parked and went into the Redmond. I had my life savings, eighty dollars in cash, on me and it made me nervous. The Redmond Apartments weren't all that safe, even if Wayne did live in splendor on the top floor. I knocked and after regarding us through the peephole a long minute, he opened the door. He was

112

wearing another tropical shirt and over it a loose, nubby-cotton jacket, eggshell-colored.

"Hi," he said, without inviting us in. His blue eyes appraised me and, more thoughtfully, Carole. "What can I do for you? Trish hasn't been by, unfortunately."

"Oh, it's not about that," I said, trying to look coy and cool at the same time. "But Trish did mention that you sometimes had access to... well, it's like this. Carole and I are going to a party tonight, and we thought it would be nice to take along a little... I've got about sixty dollars to spend... maybe half a gram?"

Wayne smiled and stepped back so we could come in. All June's talk about handguns and mass murderers hadn't exactly reassured me. Nor had reading Trish's diary. I tried to calm myself by remembering that I was nine years older than Wayne — he was just a kid, what could he do to me? Still it was harder to be engaging now than it had been the first time. I settled for businesslike. "You selling?"

"Sixty won't get you half a gram of this stuff," he said easily. "I only deal in the highest quality. I don't cut it with speed or junk — it's practically pure."

I looked at Carole; she was standing in front of one of his dog muzzle paintings, in apparent admiration.

"I could go up to seventy, but I'd have to try it first."

"No problem," he said, opening up a box on the glass coffee table and shaking out a little from a plastic bag. "You have your own razor and stuff or you want me to do it?"

"Go ahead." I wasn't exactly looking forward to it, but I didn't want him to be suspicious. We needed some reason to be there.

"It's funny," said Wayne. "The other night when you were here I wouldn't have figured you were interested in anything like this ... Trish tell you I dealt, or what?"

Careful, I thought. "Not in so many words. She mentioned getting high and I figured you were the source. That's really why I stopped by with the book. Wanted to check you out."

"Oh," he said, and gave me one of his playboy looks. It sent chills up my spine, but not the right kind. "And you liked what you saw?"

I stuck to businesslike. "I'm strictly recreational. Too expensive except for special occasions." I tried not to think of what seventy dollars would buy.

"You'll like this stuff," said Wayne. "It's worth every penny. Generally it goes for a hundred and fifty a gram, but I'll knock off ten dollars for you." He handed me a silver tooter. "Go ahead, try it."

I snorted up the line, trying not to look too amateurish, and handed the tooter to Carole, who'd wafted over to the table.

"Wow, you're some painter," she said enthusiastically. "You've really caught, like, the *essence* of the city in that one. Those skyscrapers, they really show technology out of control—and then the *animal* quality of it all..."

I guessed she meant the dog muzzles.

"Go take a close look, Pam, I mean, that's technique! Where did you study?"

Don't lay it on too thick, Carole, I warned her silently. But I wandered over anyway. The half-opened suitcase was right underneath it, and there was still something about it that bothered me.

"You really like it?" Wayne sounded pleased.

"I *love* it. It's so—primitive, but high-tech, know what I mean? You don't usually see stuff like that in Seattle."

He was warming to her by the minute and she was pouring on the sex appeal like crazy. "No really," she said, "I think you're *talented*. I'm sort of an artist myself," she added modestly. "More the *plastic* arts though...they're more *sensual*, you know."

I was in front of the painting but looking down at the suitcase. Something caught my eye. Part of a laminated card with a photo. I glanced over at Wayne and Carole. He had his hand on her arm and was explaining that he'd been influenced by the East Village school, that he didn't have time for the Seattle art scene, and Carole looked like she was eating it up. I bent over as if to tie my shoe, grabbed the card and shoved it in my pocket without looking at it. My heart was pounding as I strolled back to them.

Wayne looked over at me and something in my face must have showed, because he suddenly said, casually, but with a tightening of his mouth, "So where'd you say you met Trish? I forgot."

"Hitchhiking," I said brightly, but my mouth was dry. "Near the airport. My sister was going to Nicaragua. Boy, the airport was packed, I couldn't believe it. But you must know that—you just came back from somewhere yourself, didn't you? Where'd you say you'd been?"

"South," he smiled, staring at me.

114

"Well, you got a great tan, wherever it was," I laughed. My laugh sounded a little wild to me; it echoed slightly.

Wayne's face came closer, a little too close. His blue eyes were strangely large. I jerked back. "Whoa," I said, and laughed again, almost dementedly. Carole looked at me worriedly. I wasn't sure if I were high, or just petrified.

"Not bad, huh?" said Wayne, and then, "I'm glad you stopped by again tonight. I thought the other day that maybe Trish had given you the wrong idea about me. She's done so much dope that her thoughts tend to get a little screwed up."

I could understand how that could happen—I could feel my own thoughts screwing up dangerously.

Wayne put his hand intimately on my arm. "Earth to Pam, hey, baby, you like it, you want to make a deal?"

I closed my eyes and opened them again. With an effort I said, "Okay." I took out my wallet and handed over the bills, all of them. Carole had gone back to looking at the paintings.

"Listen Wayne," I heard myself saying. "You know the Green River killer?"

"Personally?" He laughed and went over to the stereo so his back was towards me. He put on a record by the Talking Heads. "No, I don't think I've ever met him. Why?"

"He kills young prostitutes, at least he used to...and there's this girl, Rosalie...," I stopped. Wayne didn't seem to be listening. He was moving to a track with a hard rocking beat.

"I'm worried about Trish." That wasn't what I'd meant to say.

But he stopped dancing and looked concerned. "Why is that?"

"I think she's in trouble."

"Nah," he said, coming back over to the table and wrapping up the coke. "Trish can take care of herself. What's your interest in her anyway?"

I shook my muddled head. "She's just a kid."

"So?"

"We've got to look out for kids. The streets are dangerous."

"No more dangerous than anyplace else," he soothed me.

"I'd feel better if she had a place to go," I mumbled. The coke was acting on me like a truth drug and I couldn't help it. "Oh, there's your suitcase still," I said inanely.

"Yeah, I haven't had a chance to unpack yet."

"Well I think you're really *talented*," Carole broke in, coming over and putting sharp fingernails into my arm. "And I'm going to look for your stuff in the galleries. I mean, I think you could really make it. I'm *impressed*." She started dragging me to the door.

I kept staring at the suitcase, and suddenly it struck me what was wrong. I should have seen it before. It didn't have a baggage tag. It hadn't had a tag last time either. And nobody who hadn't had time to unpack would have removed the tag. Most people left them on until the next trip rolled around. Wayne hadn't come through the airport. He'd been someplace closer. Overnight to Portland, Karl had said.

"Did you know Trish's real father lives in Portland?" I asked out of nowhere.

Wayne gave a start — or was he just dancing around? No, he was shaken somehow. I started to say something else, but I felt Carole's elbow in my side and knew that I had gone too far.

"Yeah, I think she's mentioned him a couple of times... Well, enjoy your party. And you know where I am if you or your friends decide on a little more recreation. Nice meeting you, Carole."

"This has been one of the great experiences of my life," Carole assured him fervently. "When you're famous I'll be able to say I knew you when."

But Wayne was dancing with his back to us and didn't seem to notice as we stumbled out the door.

25

You're a never-ending surprise," said Carole, when we were safely back in the street.

My high was failing me now and I felt a little foolish. In my mental script it had been Carole who was supposed to act the innocent kook, and me who was going to be cool and rational. "Well, at least I found out that Wayne has been in Portland, and that that's probably where Trish is."

"Yeah, you made it pretty clear that you made a connection, all right," Carole said. "It freaked me out the way you kept staring at his suitcase. I thought he was going to notice that I'd been standing by it too."

"I thought you were staring at his painting. I thought you liked his painting, for godssakes."

"I hope he thought so too," sighed Carole, twirling her blond lock worriedly. "You idiot! He's no more an artist than I am. No, I saw something in the suitcase, something I thought you'd be interested in."

My mind was cruising low to the ground now, ready to make a bumpy landing. "What do you mean?"

"I mean this," she said, and pulled a half of a plastic laminated card out of her linen jacket. It was part of a Washington driver's license and the name said Abby Simmons. Female, weight 125, height 5'5".

I slowly took out my own little piece of card, the half with the photograph. The memory of a slack look under a black hat with blood running out from under it returned.

It was Rosalie.

"I think you should go to the police," Carole said, as I numbly got behind the wheel of the Volvo. I was feeling sick to my stomach and I wasn't sure why. "This is evidence, Pam. You've got *evidence*."

I nodded, but part of me still resisted it. "Rosalie is dead now," I finally said. "It's Trish I'm worried about. I've got to do something..." I was realizing now how stupid I'd acted, letting Wayne know I'd figured out he took her to Portland.

"What are you trying to do, protect him or something?" Carole bounced up and down in her seat. "Call the police, Pam!"

Okay.

We drove to a phone booth and I asked to speak to the detective who'd interviewed me at the hospital, Lieutenant Logan I thought his name was. Sorry, he wasn't in. Did I want to leave a message?

"No," I said. "I'll call back later."

I went back to the car, and Carole and I drove in silence. We were supposed to be eating dinner, but she didn't mention it and I still felt sick to my stomach. I wasn't sure if it was the cocaine or the weight of Carole's — Carole of all people! — disapproval. I had handled myself badly with Wayne. I'd gotten high and said a lot of stupid things, and I might be putting Trish into an even worse situation than she was already.

And both Carole and I knew it.

Somehow we ended back up on Capitol Hill, in front of my apartment.

"Well, thanks for the date," said Carole.

I was surprised. "Don't you want to come up with me, hang out?" All of a sudden I couldn't bear the thought of being alone.

"Not really," she said. "I'll be honest with you, Pam, this wasn't fun. I thought it would be but it was just weird. And anyway, I think you need to do some serious thinking about what you're involved with here. I mean, you're not a detective and you just can't go around acting like one. Really!"

She was more serious than I'd ever known her, but I didn't want to acknowledge that she was right. All the same, the evening felt totally thrown off balance. If I hadn't been so confused and depressed and lonely I don't think I could have said what I did just then. "Carole," I said. "I want to sleep with you. Don't you want to sleep with me?"

She stiffened and her padded shoulders seemed to grow even larger; even her short blond hair appeared to bristle. "But Pam, we *work* together," she finally managed. "What can you be *thinking*?"

"You bought some coke off Wayne?" asked Beth. "You gave him eighty dollars of your hard-earned money?" She rocked back in her chair, large and unbelieving. "And here I thought you were a pretty smart cookie."

"Hardly," I said. I'd come directly to the Rainbow Center after Carole had driven off in a huff. "I think it was cut with something," I added. "My hands are shaking and I feel sick. But Beth, I think I've got an idea where Trish is, where she's hiding or where she's been taken. And I wouldn't have found out if I hadn't gone over there. I had to have some excuse." My stomach heaved.

"Put your head between your knees. I'll get you some tea and a cold cloth. The bathroom's across the hall if you need to use it."

I did. But when I finished retching, my head was finally clear. I returned to her office and gratefully accepted a cup of tea.

"Thanks, Beth. Sorry...."

"Don't mention it. I see it every day." She sighed and ran her fingers through her short strawberry hair. "So, you were saying?"

I told her what Karl had said about Wayne going to Portland and about the baggage tags and Wayne's start of surprise when I mentioned Trish's father. I told her about the two pieces of Rosalie's fake ID, how Karl had known her as Abby and said she was a real bitch. I told her I'd tried to call the detective.

"You haven't called him back?"

I shook my head. "I'm going to...but I'm more worried about

Trish, afraid the police won't find her, won't even look for her. I want to go down to Portland, Beth."

"I guess it's worth a try," she said. "There's a lot of traffic between Seattle and Portland. Things get too hot for prostitutes down there, they come up here and vice versa." She rummaged around on her crowded desk. "I know a lawyer down there if it's any help to you. Janis Glover. You might be able to stay with her and I think she could help you. Here's her number. . .she and I had an affair last fall. But we're still talking."

So she was a lesbian. Our eyes met and for a minute I forgot that I felt as emptied out and unlovely as a garbage can, that I'd just been very painfully rejected, and that my heart was eternally in Houston.

"I'll call you when I get back," I said.

"Pam?"

"Yes?"

"I'd get rid of that coke if I were you. Fast."

"It went down the toilet with my stomach lining."

"Good. I don't like to see people messing with drugs, even in the line of duty."

"Don't worry, it's not my style." I paused ruefully. "I should have known that Wayne's standards of purity were pretty goddamned low."

26

DEALING WITH THE POLICE reminded me of going to the dentist. You knew you were supposed to, but that didn't make it any more pleasant. Like dentists, detectives could make you feel small and guilty and unimportant, as if they knew what was best for you, and, most of all, as if they could solve your problems. When you went to the police it was all on their terms. You couldn't tell them what to do. You just sat there and then went away feeling numb.

At least this is how I was thinking on the late morning train to Portland. I could have driven my newly cleaned car, but I didn't think the engine would make it. And car problems in another city were something I could do without.

I had met with Lieutenant Detective Paul Logan that morning. He was the same man who had asked me questions at Harborview and he didn't seem too happy to be up so early on a Sunday. I gave him Rosalie's fake ID and told him where I got it. I told him that Wayne had been and was Trish's pimp and possibly Rosalie's and that Wayne was also a coke dealer. I had to tell Logan that I'd bought some coke, but I didn't tell him that it had turned me into a total fool. I told him about Karl though, and my underlying suspicion that he was involved in some way, and that he had known Rosalie under the name of Abby. I gave him the address of Rosalie's hotel and the addresses of Karl and Wayne.

I told Logan all this and he said, "Well, thanks for your help."

"What are you going to do now?" I asked, a little too meekly. Remove all my teeth or just fill the cavity?

"We'll be investigating," he reassured me professionally. I'll do the right thing for your mouth, Miss, and maybe we can stop this gum disease before it gets too far. Trust me.

"We'll give the Portland police her description," said Logan. Then he asked me, "Just what is your interest in this girl?"

I shook my head. I hadn't told him about Trish's diaries or the way she didn't eat green vegetables or the way Ernesto had taken to her immediately. "I'm just concerned. . . Will you let me know what you find out?"

"Give me a call later. But I can't promise anything."

So much for the police. I supposed it was only on television that they rushed over and arrested people right away. As Logan had explained, they'd have to get a search warrant for Wayne's studio, tell him his rights and allow him a lawyer. It was lucky Wayne was a dealer and not just a pimp. The police were definitely interested in drugs.

Still, I'd done my duty as a citizen, I hadn't kept anything back . . . Well, one thing. I hadn't told him that I also wondered about Rob Hemmings. I didn't want to come across as a paranoid man-hater. And besides, I had no real reason to suspect him; he'd said he hadn't seen Trish in months, that he wouldn't have anything to do with her.

At the train station, just before leaving, I tried to call Melanie, to tell her where I was going, to ask if she'd ever met Rosalie, to ask if there was any possibility Trish might have fled, on her own, to her father's house in Portland.

Rob answered the phone. "Melanie's at church," he informed me gruffly. He sounded like he'd just woken up.

"So sorry to bother you. This is Nancy Todd, the researcher from the other day. I just have a couple more questions about your stepdaughter." I continued quickly before he could interrupt. "One aspect of particular interest to us in studying adolescent delinquents is the tendency for interracial friendships to

122

develop on the street. Can you tell me if your stepdaughter had any Black friends?"

Maybe it wasn't the best approach; at any rate Rob roared into the receiver, before I even got a chance to mention Portland, "I don't know who the hell her friends are. And this is Sunday morning!" Slam went the phone.

Some people weren't at their best in the morning, I guessed.

The Coast Starlight moved smoothly southwards, through forests of dark green firs and pines, along the Sound. The snow of a week ago was gone now and it was sunny; when I looked down at the pebbles glinting under the clear water, or off at the misty blue islands, I could almost imagine it was an early spring. It was soothing, it was calming; it almost enabled me to forget where I was going, what I was coming from. Not quite. If I was anxious about Trish, I was also bummed out about Carole.

Rejected. Rejected by Carole. How had I let myself get into that position? It brought back all those feelings of last summer when Hadley had walked away, all those feelings I'd tried to erase this winter with my various affairs, affairs where I was in control, where I got the chance to back out.

How had it started with Carole; what had led me to misjudge her? That story about turning a trick maybe, her telling me she was a sexual person. I'd let my fantasies run away with me – as in, *Why would she be telling me all this if she didn't want to get it on?*

But the fantasy had been in my mind only; I'd projected on to her the image of accessibility, when all Carole had been doing was telling me a story. It was pretty embarrassing.

I hoped Penny would never get to hear about it.

It was funny, my relationship with Penny, and I could see it more clearly now she was gone. There were so many things I'd never told her, so many things I'd never wanted her to find out about me. I took it for granted that she'd be there, that she'd go first and make everything easier, that she'd protect me. Just like an older sister. In return I defended and emulated her, rarely noticing, almost never questioning that I had to hide part of myself to do it.

Once we'd been walking home from school and she'd been

123

talking about whether it was a good idea to have babies when we were young and closer to their age, or when we were older, after we'd had a chance to do something on our own. I suddenly said, out of the blue and without having thought about it, "I don't think I want to get married," and she said, "Oh, of course you will." She wasn't trying to contradict me; she was just stating what to her was obvious. And that was that. Of course I will, I thought. I'll have to, because Penny will, and she'll want to raise our children together. And I'll have to do that to, because she expects it.

Penny had accepted my becoming a lesbian the way she accepted, albeit a little skeptically, everything I did. At the same time, there was an undercurrent of sadness in our relationship now that hadn't been there before. Like the sister who loved me, she wanted me to be happy, but also, like many straight people, she wasn't sure if homosexuals really *could* be happy. And she couldn't quite understand, after having known me all these years, how I had come to such a momentous decision about my sexual and emotional life. She couldn't understand where our paths had diverged.

The truth was, our paths had diverged years ago, but she had never seen it and I had never admitted it. I wondered what my life would have been like if I hadn't had Penny as a twin. Would I have been happier, more rebellious? Somehow, from early on, Penny had locked me into her pattern, and her pattern was that of a sensible over-achiever, academically and socially. How she'd looked down on bad girls, on loose girls, on stupid girls. Girls who wore too much make-up and tight skirts, who had runs in their pantyhose and reeked of perfume, girls who had hickies on their necks and failed their tests. I wouldn't have dared to have a friend from that crowd, even though there was always something about them that fascinated and attracted me.

Stella was a girl in my tenth grade drama class. She was Italian, with thick, open-pored skin, dark brown curly hair and a wide, sensual mouth, always laughing. She hung around with the seniors and went out on dates and smoked cigarettes in the parking lot. I had a terrible crush on her until that day Penny remarked, in passing, "There's something really whorish about Stella, don't you think?"

Had she really said that?

Yes. And I had agreed. Stella, whom I had admired as a gypsy and a bohemian, would never become *my* friend.

Maybe Penny was aware of some tendency in me to slip down the same path. She was always lecturing me about combing my hair, not putting on too much mascara, ironing my clothes. Naturally. It reflected on her. She tamed any little wildness I might have had and I acquiesced. Because I loved and admired her, because I was used to her telling me what to do; because not being like her meant being myself. And sometimes that still frightened me.

I *still* loved and admired her. I missed her terribly down there in Nicaragua, and I couldn't imagine life, past, present or future, without her.

All the same — for one of the first times in my life, as the train rolled calmly on its way to Portland — I felt I was glad not to have her around.

Janis Glover was waiting in the train station for me. She was a slim, athletic woman in her mid-thirties, dressed in an expensive maroon training suit. Her flyaway dark hair was tucked behind her ears and held in place with an elastic maroon headband, and she had two little no-nonsense gold hoops in her ears. She looked like she'd just put down her squash racket.

"Good trip?" she asked, without waiting for an answer. "My car's out front." She hurried me through the marble and wood lobby out to a new MG and tossed my bag in the trunk.

"How's Beth?" she asked, revving the motor and tearing through the parking lot.

"Fine, she sends her regards." I couldn't imagine two more unlike people and wondered how they'd ever gotten together. Beth was a large, compassionate bed of calm compared to this straight-backed chair of efficiency.

"That's good," said Janis and dropped the subject. "You know Portland at all?"

"Not very well..."

Before I knew it, she was giving me a rapid tour of the city's streets, complete with past and present history, a rundown on the city's politics and all her own opinions on its politicians.

"That's the new Justice Center and there's the Portland Building with the statue of Portlandia, no, it's on the other side, you can't see it," and then we were racing over a steel-girded bridge that spanned the Willamette River.

MGs are small and low and I couldn't see much of anything. I gave up trying to understand or keep up with her, until she suddenly pulled up at a pleasant-looking little house on a quiet sidestreet. Then she turned to me and with a change of tone, almost a break in her voice, said, "So is Beth really doing okay?"

27

Bᴜᴛ ᴄᴀɴ ʏᴏᴜ ɪᴍᴀɢɪɴᴇ two people more incompatible? Her incessant smoking and her coffee and her pink bedroom slippers. And her life! She's available to those kids at the center day and night, and her house is a total shambles, just like her office. Newspapers and cats everywhere, dishes stacked in the sink, grunge in the bathroom. I've never met such a slob."

We sat across from each other in Janis' combination dining room and work space. The phone had been ringing continually. Janis was as impatient and quick in her phone conversations as in her movements, punctuating her rapid-fire instructions and explanations with finger-snapping and foot-drumming. While she talked I looked around at the obsessive neatness of the room. Her life, like Beth's, was filled with papers and folders, but they were all labelled and stored away. Two file cabinets rose in the corner; the desk drawers were marked and the desk top was nearly empty save for a handsome leather blotter/calendar and a rosebud in a crystal vase. On a small wicker bed quivered a short-haired terrier, as sleek and wiry as Janis.

Hanging up the phone, Janis returned to her subject. "Social workers! I loathe social workers! I could never have imagined getting involved with a bleeding heart social worker. That's not my approach to the world at all. Sure, I'm interested in my clients — but most of them are weak, manipulative people who continually screw up their lives and who probably deserve to be locked up, even though I do my best to get them off."

The phone rang again and while Janis answered it, I thought of Beth's description of their meeting. "It was at a conference I was helping to organize. We'd asked this hot shot lawyer from Portland to come. We were all a little nervous about it. She'd just gotten a battered woman off for killing her husband, so we figured she'd know what she was talking about, but no one knew whether she was a feminist or just a good lawyer. Janis turned up in a three-piece suit and gave a brilliant talk. I was sort of assigned to take care of her, and I did everything wrong. Took her to a restaurant where she couldn't eat anything on the menu, things like that." Beth had groaned at the memory. "And I ran out of gas. I remember standing on the freeway in the pouring rain, trying to get somebody to stop, while Janis just sat in the car, polite and more and more exasperated. I knew she thought I was a nerd, a complete nerd."

"And this whole prostitution thing," Janis said, hanging up and bouncing around on the chair. "You can't just go around feeling sorry for them and thinking they got a raw deal in life. A lot of them make more money than I do and would be perfectly satisfied with life if the cops didn't harass them."

A severe expression came into her light hazel eyes with their bristly lashes, and a straight, short furrow appeared between her thin eyebrows. "Who am I — or any feminist — to decide whether prostitution is a good or bad thing for the women who do it? This wave of puritanism — it's got women doing exactly what they did a hundred years ago, getting all worked up about their fallen sisters, trying to save them. No wonder hookers laugh at us — with our liberal diatribes about how men use women as sex objects. Most prostitutes I've met feel like they're the ones in control, using men to get back what's owing to them economically. Hell if they care about being poor and pure!"

The phone rang again and Janis leapt to answer it; she poured forth a flood of legalese to someone on the other end. It was starting to exhaust me just to watch her, much less listen to her. I could see how she won her cases—probably everyone left the courtroom on stretchers.

"I always thought Janis would be the one to break it off," Beth had said. "That she'd decide I was just too flaky. But, in fact, it was me. She'd started on the theme of me moving to Portland and she wouldn't let up. Maniacal persistence and brilliant arguments—those are what make her such a fine lawyer—but it's wearing. I felt like a prisoner in the dock. 'Let's examine your reasons for not wanting to move to Portland.' I'd give her my reasons—I like my job, I have a lot of friends in Seattle, my son, who lives with his father, is here—and she'd demolish them one by one. It was second nature to her."

"You know what I should do," said Janis when she got off the phone. "I should introduce you to a real prostitute, a professional." She went over and inspected her rose for signs of withering and looked pleased with herself, then suddenly snapped her fingers. "I've got to get back to the office. I'm up to my ears in a big case. Back in a minute after I change. Can I drop you anyplace? Here's a map of Portland."

She vanished into her bedroom, leaving me wondering what to do now, where I should start. Beth had warned me that Janis wouldn't have much time for me, that her life was as tightly scheduled as the arrivals and departures board at a major airport. But she'd also said that Janis had a good heart and would be supportive if I told her clearly what I wanted.

I had tried to be clear on the phone last night; I had tried to sound focused and practical. But I hadn't been sure that she believed me. The search for Trish had sounded to me like a wild goose chase even as I described it.

"Sure you can come," she'd said. "But it's not going to be easy. Portland's a big city and I don't know how much help I can give you."

I heard her running water in the bathroom, and hastily dialed the number of Art Margolin from Trish's diary. There was no answer. I could try again later or go to the house, but other than that what else was there to do but to start walking around, hoping I ran into Trish? Beth had given me the phone numbers of social workers, of juvenile agencies, but it was Sunday. If only I knew who had brought Trish to Portland and what she might be doing here. Would she be tricking, out making money for

Wayne? Or hiding? And would whoever brought her to Portland get to her before I could?

The terrier looked at me and wagged her tail; I looked at the terrier and realized that I'd gone off and forgotten Ernesto.

I called June at home. "Hiya."

"Is this long-distance, Pam?" she asked suspiciously. "I want to know where you are, right now!"

"Managua," I said. "Can you hear me? It's incredibly warm down here. Sure beats Seattle."

"Come off it, Pam," she said impatiently, but there was an undertone of worry. It pleased me to realize how unpredictable she thought me.

"I'm in Portland actually. I think Trish is here. I'm looking for her...so dinner's off tonight, tell Carole, and...I need someone to feed Ernesto while I'm gone."

"I'm sure as hell not going to feed Ernesto...what do you think, a business runs itself? You come back here right away!"

"I can't, June, I've got to find her. I think someone may have brought her down here. I've got to ask her some questions, help her."

There was a pause. "Well, at least you didn't die from an overdose. I guess I can be thankful for that. But you be back by Wednesday, hear? Cause we got a big job coming up and I need some help too."

"Then you'll feed Ernesto? Thanks a million, June, you're great."

"I'm great till Wednesday," she warned. "Then I'm mad."

Janis returned, in a three-piece suit, a crisp white shirt and blue tie. She carefully placed some papers in her briefcase.

"Decided what you want to do?"

"Just walk around, I guess. Try to see Trish's father..."

"Good," she said. "I'll drop you downtown. Tonight I'll show you where the prostitutes hang out."

"Thanks," I started to say, but she interrupted me.

"We'll eat dinner at home, if that's all right with you. I hope you can handle vegetarian food." She added severely, "Beth couldn't."

28

PORTLANDIA BENT DOWN from her ledge two stories up, golden bronze, leaning forward on one knee, grasping a trident in one hand and stretching the other out to me on the ground, as if she wanted to give me a boost up. Her shoulders were massive and powerful, her long hair was flung back and she gleamed like molten lava in the light of the afternoon sun. Behind her the windows reflected and deepened the color of the bright blue sky. You didn't often see statues that showed a woman's strength, not her fragility, that showed a woman who looked like she could really do something for you.

The day was cold and the wind bit my neck. In my haste to get out of Seattle I'd forgotten my muffler and hat, though thankfully not my blue mittens.

I stood there looking at Portlandia, thinking over what Janis had said about feminists and prostitution.

In the car I'd told her, "You make it sound like prostitutes, the ones you've met, have a choice. But it doesn't feel like that to me. A lot of them are young girls who've been victims of sexual abuse and they go on being victimized." I was remembering the despair and corrupted sensibility of Trish's diary, and how the girls in the group had talked about not feeling anything.

"Even victims have a choice," said Janis, driving very fast. "Survival is a choice and prostitution is a means of economic survival. Don't get me wrong. There's a psychological price to be paid. But you pay a price when you work at McDonald's for minimum wage and have to wear those ridiculous uniforms. Society punishes prostitutes and so of course they suffer. But it doesn't have to be that way."

"You think prostitution should be legalized then?"

"Not legalized!" The MG shot over the bridge like a bullet fired low to the ground. "That would mean the state would intervene and control it. It's legal in Germany, for instance, and what you get are Eros Hotels, legalized brothels that make huge profits for the men who own them. The women are practically prisoners— they see dozens of men a day, they can't set their own hours, some of them can't even leave their rooms." Janis impatiently tucked a wisp of brown hair behind her ears and raced through a yellow light. "No, I'm talking about just leaving prostitutes alone, about decriminalization. Just stop arresting them. Do you know that thirty percent of all women in the prison system are in for prostitution? Do you know how much it costs to arrest and try each woman? The city of Portland spent over three-quarters of a million dollars last year arresting and rearresting prostitutes. It's just a waste of money."

She stopped at a red light, stopped on a dime.

"What's the crime if a woman sleeps with a man for money? He gets what he wants sexually, she gets what she needs economically. Why should the state in the guise of public morality intervene? It's all hypocrisy anyway. Everyone knows that prostitution will continue no matter how many laws you make or unmake. The politicians are some of the prostitutes' best customers."

"But that's just it," I said, trying to grab hold of an argument and feeling almost defeated before I began by her energy. "Why *is* the institution of prostitution always seen as something that's always been there and always will be? It just feeds into the myth that men are these insatiable sexual creatures whose needs have got to be met. Legally or illegally, that's not really the question. As long as we accept the idea that men need prostitutes, we accept the idea that women are responsible for men's sexuality.

Women are responsible for their *own* sexuality — why aren't men? Why is men's sexuality something that has to be catered to and supplied on demand as a 'service'?"

Janis screeched to a stop in front of the new Justice Center. "You're bucking thousands of years of history with that little question."

"Well, so is feminism," I said as I squeezed out.

"Don't forget, it's vegetarian food tonight. So stock up on your hamburgers this afternoon."

She roared away with a wave, leaving me standing on the sidewalk muttering, "But you didn't tell me where to find the goddamn McDonald's."

I wandered around the river city, up one street and down the next, not sure if I was looking for Trish or just looking, and finally ended up in Burnside. This was Portland's skid road, now in the process of being renovated. Expensive restaurants and boutiques nestled next to abandoned storefronts and corner grocers; in front of them small crowds of street people hung out, or stood in line for a hot meal at one of the missions. It reminded me of photos I'd seen of the Depression: long lines of men, beaten down and patient, waiting for the soup kitchen to open. There weren't many women and only a few teenage girls, most of them Black or Indian. It was odd; when I thought of Depression photographs I mainly remembered images of men. Where had the women been? Where were they now? At home with the kids, in shelters or cheap rooming houses. Just as needy, but invisible.

Some of Burnside's streets hadn't been touched by gentrification and were a lonely series of boarded-up shops and miserable taverns. But on Sixth I saw a small storefront with a frosting of old Christmas decorations in the window and a sign: Sisters of the Road Cafe.

I walked across the street and went inside, a little hesitantly. It wasn't much: a counter and tables for about twenty customers. At the counter was a woman and a few men. The men were dressed in layers of torn clothing, in shoes with worn heels and flapping soles; unbrushed, unwashed, with scraggly beards. The woman was better looking, but she had a rundown air. It was hard to know how old she was — twenty-five, thirty-five. She was wearing a skirt and thin sweater, high patent leather boots that were cracked at the toe.

"The special's chili for eighty-five cents," the waitress who came over to my table said. "We've also got rice, beans and cheese." She was stocky in a faded chef's apron over jeans and a plaid shirt, one of those people who seem firmly rooted to the ground, like a small tree. Her dark hair was long and bushy and she had heavy eyebrows and a generous mouth.

"I'll take a bowl of the chili, I guess. And some coffee."

I kept looking at the woman at the counter. She was slumped over a cup of coffee, her peroxided hair pulled back into a limp ponytail; her face, from my angle, was sweet, soft and puffy, like a bowl of whipped cream just starting to settle. She had a fresh bruise under one eye.

I was still thinking about my conversation with Janis. I wondered what she really felt, emotionally, about prostitution. I wondered what I felt.

Powerful, Carole had said. Nasty. It was both, it was neither. It was all tangled up in my mind with legend and literature. Japanese geishas, *Irma la Douce*, Colette's demi-monde, Xaviera Hollander, and Lola Montez. Seductive images that warred with other pictures: diseased, nameless hags standing in doorways, displayed in street windows, greasy, toothless women reeking of gin. History and novels gave you both: the myth of the *grand horizontal*, sensual, charming, clever, and the myth of the harlot, the scarlet woman, the whore, the most pitiful and despicable creature on earth. Men said you were one or the other; somehow you suspected you might be both. All the same you chose. Good girl, bad girl.

The waitress came over with my chili.

"You from around here?"

"Seattle."

"Just traveling?"

"No. I'm looking for a girl, a friend of mine, a kid really."

She nodded, straightening a chair slightly. "We don't get too many street kids in here. Some, but mainly it's the Burnside regulars."

I felt a sudden urge to confide, but I didn't know what. Maybe that I was a little lost and lonely, that I didn't know where Trish was or why Rosalie had to die, or what would happen to Trish if

I didn't find her.

She stood there waiting, sturdy and gentle.

"Why Sisters of the Road?" I finally asked.

"We had a project called Boxcar Berthas for transient women and the cafe came out of that. We wanted to make a safe place for women." The waitress smiled and the smile was warm and easy and kind. She wasn't going to press me. "Boxcar Bertha was a hobo who wrote a book, *Sister of the Road*. She was into helping other women, she knew what it was like. Enjoy your chili."

She went back to the counter and started refilling coffee cups, joking a little with the men. The woman with the bruise didn't talk; she seemed sunk in some private hell. Exhaustion perhaps, or misery.

"Fucking bitch!"

The door had swung open and a small Black man in built-up shoes and a suit with wide lapels and padded shoulders stood there. "I been looking all over town for you. Come on."

The woman at the counter slumped over more deeply and didn't turn around.

"What's the problem?" the waitress said calmly. She came out from behind the counter, wiping her hands on her apron and stood, solidly planted, between him and the woman.

"Shut up, bitch! This is between me and Louise. Come on, get up and get over here, before I have to drag you." His face was mean and angry; his voice seethed.

The woman at the counter didn't move. The men at the counter didn't either. I half got up and said, "You want me to call the police?"

"No," said the waitress. She was still standing in the middle of the cafe, large and immovable with her bushy dark hair fanning out over her shoulders. Her voice was mild. "Calm down, mister. Just calm down now. You can go in the kitchen if you want, Louise."

Louise turned slightly from the counter. "I'm not going with you, Earl." She was frightened but aggrieved. "Not after what you did."

"You fucking get off that seat and get out here right away. You'll go where I tell you to go." The man didn't come any nearer, though, and the anger in his face retreated a little, leaving a contempt that was uncertain and cajoling. "Come on, Louise, don't let this bitch tell you what to do. She doesn't know about you and me."

"Earl," said the waitress, very calm and clear. "Louise is having a cup of coffee. She can stay here as long as she wants."

She didn't tell him to go, she didn't threaten him. She just stood there.

"I'm not leaving, Earl, forget it," muttered Louise. "Not after what you did."

All of a sudden his bluster left him. He looked furious, but defeated. "Fucking white bitch," he said and turned and slammed out the door.

I sat down again.

The waitress sighed and went back behind the counter. I expected her to talk to Louise, to ask her what had happened, to tell her where she could go for help. She didn't. She said, as if to herself, "This cafe is a safe place, it's always going to be a safe place."

I ate my chili. I stayed a little longer than I needed to. Louise was still sitting there when I left.

29

Trish's FATHER, ART MARGOLIN, didn't live far from Janis, in a modest frame house with a neatly kept yard. It was almost sunset when I found the address; the front windows glowed like bars of toffee and a wind chime tinkled a little above the door. A large yellow cat sat on a jute mat on the porch.

My heart lifted as I saw the house. Maybe I'd been worried for nothing. Maybe Trish was here; maybe her father had taken her in and was even now doing something to help and protect her.

I rang the doorbell expectantly. A small Japanese-American woman in a print dress and cardigan sweater opened up.

"I'm Pam Nilsen, from Seattle. Are you Mrs. Margolin?"

She nodded. She wore glasses and a prim, judgmental look.

"I'm looking for Art Margolin. I'd like to talk to him about his daughter, Trish."

She hesitated slightly, then asked me in. "He's in the kitchen."

The house bore unmistakable signs of children. A rocking horse in the living room, toys on the stairs, a baby carriage in the hall. Two kids, a boy of five or six and a girl somewhat younger, were in the kitchen with a tall, heavily built man. He was stirring a pot on the stove and looking at a cookbook while talking to them absentmindedly. A radio was on and the whole scene was exceedingly domestic.

Better and better, I thought; if Trish weren't here, maybe she should be. Why hadn't she ever talked about her father?

"Art, this is Pam Nilsen from Seattle. She wants to know something about Patricia."

Art's big distracted features focused on me. He had bushy graying eyebrows and a receding hairline; his mouth was slack and unfinished, as if a mason had slapped a smear of mortar between his jowls, and it was still wet and grayish-pink.

"Why, what's happened to her?"

"She's disappeared from Seattle. I thought she might have come here. I'm a friend of hers."

Art and his wife looked at each other. "She wouldn't have come here," said the woman matter-of-factly. She shooed the children out into the hall; they stared at me worriedly as they went.

"She might, Judy," Art said. "She might have changed. Is she in trouble?" He sounded almost hopeful.

"I think she might be," I said. "Has she been to visit before?"

"Up until about six months ago she used to come down sometimes," Judy said. "But we haven't seen her since last September or October."

"We always had a good time," said Art eagerly, putting down his spoon and extending an arm around his small wife's shoulders. "She helped with the kids and around the house. We went camping once with the Bible study class."

"She accepted the Lord Jesus Christ into her heart, but then she repudiated him," Judy said. "Evil ways overcame her and the Devil entered her soul."

As if that were a sign, I suddenly became aware that the voice on the radio was that of an evangelical preacher, and that there was a bright little placard over the kitchen table that read, "Trust in the Lord."

"If she's in trouble she may be ready to take the Lord back into her heart again, Judy," Art reproved his wife with a gentle smack of his mortared lips. "We would never turn her away."

"Did you have a fight last fall?"

Judy's face went pinched and hard. "Patricia treated us like fools. She showed no respect for her father or me. She refused to go to church."

"I know she was having a hard time at home with her mother and stepfather and in the foster homes. She'd been on drugs and arrested and in jail," Art said. "But the Lord is willing to forgive and forget. We can too, Judy."

Judy looked as if forgiving came harder to her than to her husband. "I was afraid for the children," she said sanctimoniously. "Afraid she'd be a bad influence." She glanced in the direction of the hall.

"She's young, Judy, she's a troubled soul." Art went back to stirring his pot. I couldn't see his face. "Very troubled."

"Art is an extremely loving person," said Judy, with a degree of resentment. "He had a hard time seeing that Patricia was in the power of the Devil."

The radio evangelist was building up to a crackling crescendo.

"What could she be doing in Portland?" Art worried. "Why hasn't she come to us?"

"She probably will," I tried to reassure him, even though I knew now that I couldn't hope to find Trish with these fundamentalists, one of whom, at least, suspected her of being on the Devil's payroll.

I left them my address and phone number at Janis' and Judy gave me a couple of tracts from a pile on the kitchen table.

"If you see her," said Art, looking at his cookbook again, "Tell her we forgive her and that the Lord will too."

It was twilight when I left the Margolins, that eerie time of day that seems darker than real night. A cold mist had moved in from the river like a spray from a can of quick-freeze propellant, and I felt very conscious of being in a neighborhood I didn't know, in a city I didn't know.

When I heard quick, heavy steps behind me I almost ran, but stopped to glance back an instant. It was Art Margolin, out of breath, huge in an orange parka and tennis shoes, coming after me.

"Wait," he called. "Please wait."

I waited, underneath the nearest streetlight.

"What is it?" I asked more brusquely than I meant. He'd scared the shit out of me.

"I . . ." he stopped and wiped his forehead. "A little out of shape, I guess . . ." He wet his big, cement-like lips and said, "After you left, I thought, well, I thought there's something you ought to know. It's not just like we said in there, I mean that Patti stopped coming to see us because of religion and all."

He stared at me mournfully, pathetically, a large dog that's done something wrong, and hopes desperately to be forgiven. I didn't know why he'd chosen me.

"Why did she stop coming?" I prompted him, when he fell silent.

"It was something that happened a long time ago, when Patti was small . . ." He wiped his forehead and started again. "You see, when I was married to Melanie, before I found Jesus, I had a problem. Judy knows and Jesus has forgiven me. I'd never do it again. It was the Devil in me, I guess. I don't really understand it, but you see, when Patti was real young, only four or five . . ."

I unconsciously held up a hand to stop him. I could guess the rest.

"Melanie found out and got a divorce. She didn't press charges, thank the Lord, and Patti never seemed to remember it. I came to Portland and started over. I found Jesus — and Judy. She believed me when I said I'd never do it again. And I never have. It's like a bad dream."

The cold mist swirled around us, each droplet a mosquito of cold, biting my exposed skin.

"But Trish did remember," I said slowly. "That's why she never talked about you to me."

"It was only a few times." He was begging me to understand. "I never would have hurt Patti. I loved her so much. And she started coming to visit when she was ten sometimes. Her mother saw I'd changed. I have changed."

I remembered Trish's diary entry. The girl in her group, Julianne, who'd talked about her incest experience and confronted her father. It hadn't been Wayne Trish had decided to confront. It had been Art.

"So she came here last September and told you she remembered, and you told her . . . what?"

"The Lord forgive me," Art whispered. "I told her she was imagining it, that it never happened. I couldn't face her knowing what I'd done to her. I didn't tell Judy about our conversation. I let her think Patti left because of the religious conflicts."

And Trish had gone back to Seattle, to Wayne, to the only person she thought cared about her.

Art fumbled in his parka pocket. "After she left, I found this diary. It was only then that I realized what I'd done to her. I went up to Seattle, I've been up there many times looking for her. I want to tell her I'm sorry."

"It may be too late."

"Please, take this," he pressed the square fat volume into my hands. "And when you see her, give it to her and tell her I'm sorry. I need her forgiveness."

30

JANIS WAS AT HOME WHEN I RETURNED, cooking dinner: Szechuwan Tofu Triangles with Triple Pepper Sauce. Now back in her maroon training suit, her flyaway brown hair tucked firmly behind her ears, she poured us each a glass of nutty Spanish sherry and directed me to sit at her kitchen table and chop salad vegetables. "Not too large, not too small." The knife she gave me was very sharp, and I attacked the peppers with a will, glad to feel useful for once today.

"Did you find out anything?" she asked.

"Not really." I'd put away the diary to read later, not ready to face it yet, not ready to talk to Janis about what I had learned from Art. Was there any possibility that he had killed Rosalie and abducted Trish? I doubted it strongly; all the same, he was one more man in Trish's life who had hurt her. "I'll try some agencies tomorrow," I said, a little hopelessly.

"Don't give up yet," Janis said, attacking the soft white cake of tofu, slicing it expertly into triangles. "I talked to Dawn Jacobs, a prostitute I know, and she's coming over this evening. She'll be more interesting than the social workers." She threw the tofu in the sizzling oil of the wok. "Social work doesn't change anything, you know. The only way to change anything is through the law."

Janis' mind clearly was still running on her conflicts with Beth.

"So that's how you help people—through the law?"

"Who said anything about helping! Most people deserve the stupid messes they get into. I don't want to help them—I want to win my cases!" She removed the tofu from the wok with a slotted spoon and put it to drain in a paper towel. "Don't think I'm an awful person. I *have* ended up helping a lot of people, especially women. But it's not always because I think they're right—it's because I need to prove to myself and the rest of the world that women have a right to win. And the only way I see for establishing that is through legal means, through case after case of precedents."

"That sounds pretty idealistic."

"No way. I'm hard-headed realism itself." She sprang lithely over to check my chopping technique, criticized it, and then whipped together a salad dressing in the space of a few minutes.

It seemed to be my fate in life always to be surrounded by hard-headed realists. She and Penny and June would get along just fine.

"What'd you get your degree in anyway?" she asked me suddenly.

"Political science. But I don't use it. I'm in business—when I'm not being an amateur detective."

"So you've never thought of becoming a helping professional?"

"I don't think professional helping would suit me. Too many forms."

"Then what's your motive for looking for this girl? I don't get it. Even Beth, the great bleeding heart herself, wouldn't leave her job to go wandering around Portland searching for someone."

I didn't think Janis was the kind of person who'd understand a moral imperative or a concept of help that didn't include a solution. I wasn't sure I understood it myself.

I took a sip of sherry and shook my head. "Maybe I'm trying to establish a precedent too."

At eight o'clock, Dawn Jacobs, Janis' "real" prostitute, came over for tea and cake. Janis had once defended her on a blackmail charge ("Don't worry, she didn't do it.") and they had kept in touch.

I was nervous and didn't know what to expect. Which version of the myth would she be? A slinky, sexy call girl or a hard-faced bitter streetwalker with a ruthless habit? And how was meeting her going to help me find Trish?

I never imagined that Dawn would be in her mid-thirties, a little overweight, with frosted curly hair and an open, lively expression, or that she would be wearing running shoes and a sweatshirt decorated with lines of cows grazing back and forth. She could have been the loquacious lady at my dry cleaner's, or my mother's best friend when I was growing up.

"Janis, you sweetheart! Look at this cake! You can't tell me nobody wants you for their permanent girlfriend. Rich, cute, and she can cook." Dawn settled herself on the couch with a sigh of satisfaction and crossed her plump legs. "Cut me a big slice, forget the diet. How does she do it?" Dawn turned to me with a broad smile. "I saw her—she worked twelve hours a day on my case and still she had time to bake me cookies. She doesn't sleep, I know it. That's her secret."

Janis looked pleased, though she tried to be offhand. "Oh, I'm just organized."

"You're organized like the Pentagon," Dawn laughed, lolling comfortably back on the couch with a huge slice of carrot cake. "Only you're the generals and the staff all rolled into one. So, Pam," she said, without a pause, "I hear you're looking into prostitution in Portland?"

"I'm actually looking for a girl who's a prostitute...." What had Janis told her anyway? That I was writing a book?

"Well, I'm here to tell you everything you want to know," she said, exactly like the lady at the dry cleaner's before she launched into the story of her son's asthma and her daughter's allergies and how she had refused to accept what the first doctor said, but gone looking for the best specialist in town. "Don't be shy. I love to puncture people's preconceptions. We're not monsters, we're not all on heroin and we do lead happy, fulfilled lives, at least about as often as so-called regular people do. You want to know how I started?" she asked, with her mouth full. "I was twenty-eight, divorced, had two kids and was trying to put myself through college. I'd never had a job before, couldn't type, couldn't do diddlyshit. And I was studying English! I wanted to be an English teacher, if you can believe it. What a lucrative profession!

"So I'm in this bar one night with a girlfriend of mine, somebody I've known for years, and as usual I'm complaining about how I don't have any money, and I say, 'Bonnie, how do you do it? You can't manage to hold down a regular job and yet you always seem to look good and have what you want. Are you shoplifting or what?' Bonnie hems and haws a little, but we've been drinking and she's pretty loosened up and all of a sudden she tells me that she's been turning tricks for two years. A friend of mine! 'Why didn't you tell me, Bonnie?' 'I thought you'd look down on me,' she says.

"'Well, I didn't know what to say. 'Look,' she says. 'What's so different about what I'm doing and what you did when you were married? You had to get down on your hands and knees to get any money out of Alan, you slept with him when you didn't feel like it just to keep him happy so's he'd keep supporting you — and he didn't even do that! What's the difference to what I did working as a clerk or secretary? I had to sell myself eight hours a day for a measly salary — *and* I had to put up with my boss making off-color jokes and pretend to laugh if I didn't want to get fired. This way I make a hell of a lot of money in less time and I don't have to put up with any shit.'

"Well, I tell you," Dawn said, cutting herself another piece of carrot cake. "It certainly made me think. And I decided to try it out. I thought maybe johns were weirdos, but they weren't. Most of them are married businessmen who're bored but don't want the hassles of an affair. A lot of them just want someone to talk to. So I stuck with it. I didn't have to worry about daycare cause I could work three or four nights a week and get a babysitter. It's easy work and I've got my regular customers, had some of them for years."

Dawn chattered with the jovial impersonality of a woman long accustomed to speaking her mind, a woman whose public self seemed effortlessly joined to her private self, so that she could talk about the most intimate things in the most unconcerned way possible. My mother's best friend, Nancy, has been like that. She used to keep us in stitches with stories of her fights with her husband; it was only long afterwards that my mother found out she'd been battered for years.

145

"Now I know you're going to say, 'It can't be all that great,'" Dawn said, as if reading my mind. "And I can't pretend that I haven't met a couple of sickos over the years. And sure, I'm not always in the mood to listen to some john tell me about his sexual troubles with his wife. But I make a habit of separating myself from it. You have to," Dawn said, and the cows shrugged in unison on her chest. "You never let them kiss your mouth, for instance. It's a business like any other, like waitressing, like selling vacuum cleaners. I just wish that people would realize that hookers perform a real service and we deserve a little respect."

She was convincing, but something in me balked. "You think there'll always be prostitution then?"

Dawn chuckled good-naturedly, pouring sugar into her tea. "Men aren't going to change, honey. And it's men who're on top, like it or not. All we can do is stick together and try to get fair treatment." She stirred her cup and sipped. The cows rose and fell. "Like those prostitutes' unions over in France and England. That's the way to go. They've got the right idea. We shouldn't be treated like criminals. Nobody should."

"But what about kids in prostitution?" I asked. "The girl I'm looking for is only fifteen. She didn't make the choice as an adult, she was pushed into it."

"If there were strong hookers' unions we could do something about that," said Dawn firmly, succumbing to another slice. "Set an age limit, regulate. Keep them off the streets until they were eighteen. Not that I think anybody should be on the streets if they can help it. It's too dangerous."

I felt as if I were arguing with a factory worker about immigrants and aliens taking away American jobs. "What do you do about the fact that men seem to want younger and younger girls all the time? And what do you do about the teenagers out there on the streets right now?"

Dawn shrugged and changed tactics. "Excuse me for asking, but are you a feminist?"

I admitted I was.

"Well, I tell you, I've got a real bone to pick with feminists." Her lively expression closed up and she fixed me with an accusing stare. "They could be out there supporting us, instead of sitting home writing articles for and against pornography. I've seen some of those articles and I can tell you they practically make me

146

ashamed to call myself a woman." Dawn put down her teacup with a bang. "There's a woman right here in Portland who calls herself a feminist – I hear she even used to be a lesbian – and she's involved with some neighborhood organizing group. She's given interviews to the newspapers saying people should get together to patrol their neighborhoods to keep out hookers and other un-desirables. She says they should carry *walkie-talkies*, like god-damn vigilantes or something. What I want to know is why feminists think they're so much better than we are, why they can't see this from our point of view."

"That'll be the day," said Janis, stretching her legs and flexing her biceps. "They'd rather pass laws against sexuality than admit they have anything in common with sex workers."

I was silent. It was the old good girl/bad girl theme again. And somehow I was still stuck on the side of the good girls.

"You think about this, Pam," said Dawn, polishing off the last of the carrot cake. "If you want to find this girl you've got to decide where you stand. Because she's not going to listen to you if she thinks you're judging her. I wouldn't." She stood up and the cows on the sweatshirt straightened up too. "But now I'm late. I'm visiting old Mr. Taylor at his hotel. He comes in from Hermiston once a month to have a nice time." She stroked Janis' wispy brown hair. "Janis, I didn't *mean* to eat all your carrot cake. It was just too *good!*"

"You look a little shattered," Janis said, after Dawn had gone.

"I feel like I've just had a shock treatment," I admitted. "What kind of theoretical arguments can you put up against the reality of someone's life?"

"You can't," said Janis, piling the dessert plates together and meticulously brushing the crumbs off the couch where Dawn had been sitting. "You have to change theory to fit reality. All the same," she added thoughtfully. "I wouldn't give Dawn the last word on the subject. She's got an investment in what she does, she's not going to let anybody feel sorry for her. And why should they? But it's not quite as easy for her as she'd like you to believe. She's been threatened and ripped off, beaten up more than a few times. You can talk all you want about a prostitutes' union and women controlling it themselves. But it's never going to be a safe profession. Because men aren't safe."

I followed Janis out to the kitchen. "She didn't seem all that interested in girls on the street."

"No, she wasn't as helpful as I thought she'd be." Janis ran water in the sink and washed the dishes rapidly. "But I forgot what an incredibly rigid hierarchy prostitution has. The mistresses of wealthy men look down on the hotel call girls who look down on the women who work in massage parlors. Everybody looks down on the street hookers. And no doubt about it, young prostitutes threaten Dawn. Sure," Janis drained the sink. "She's not getting any younger and new women who think it's a far-out way to make a lot of money are moving in all the time. She may be saving some money, but she's probably only got five more years. Cautious as she is, she's got a record—who's going to hire her? And prostitution doesn't give you a pension or social security."

"Yesterday you were telling me prostitution would be a great profession if they could just get the cops off their backs."

"Sometimes I'm as full of bullshit as my clients." Janis whistled to her terrier and the dog came running. "Come on," she said to me. "Now that we're in the mood, let's go look for Trish."

31

JANIS DIDN'T KNOW HOW TO WALK, only to run. Winded almost immediately, I could barely manage to keep up with her and the wiry little terrier. The night was cold and starry with a moon like a saucer of frozen milk low on the horizon. I missed my hat and muffler.

"This is Sandy Boulevard. Union and Sandy are the main prostitution scenes, lots of motels and pick-ups. If Trish is working she's likely to be here. Tell me what she looks like again."

"Tallish, big breasts, skinny arms and legs. Streaked blond hair, a triangular little face. She might be wearing a white leather jacket and a black hat," I gasped. Even by speaking I seemed to have fallen behind Janis.

There were a number of girls and women out tonight, but none fitting that description. Some were very young-looking, barely dressed up; others fitted the more conventional image of the streetwalker. They were Black, white, in pairs or alone. They walked slowly, they smoked, they got into cars. They returned.

I tried to get glimpses of the men who were driving by, the men who picked them up. Was one of them Wayne? Or Rob or Karl, keeping an eye on Trish, looking for her?

Or just workers and businessmen, out for the hunt, their faces pale and shadowy, leering under the street lights. I tried to think what it felt like to be a man looking for a hooker, what he wanted, what he needed.

He might come home from work after a bad day at the office. The boss had told him to do a report over. He wanted to quit but where would he go? House payments, car payments, doctor bills, credit stretched to the limit. Maybe his wife wasn't home, maybe she was at a potluck with women from work, maybe she'd left him a note, "Dinner in freezer, just heat up." He'd have a beer or a scotch, watch television, feel pissed off. At work, at his wife, at women in general, at life in general.

Maybe getting into his car to look for a girl was something he did all the time; maybe it was just this once. From frustration, from anger. From a feeling he was lonely, and getting old, and that his wife didn't understand him.

Maybe he'd thought about it all day, maybe it was just a sudden titillating whim. It wasn't all that risky, but maybe it was, maybe he wanted the risk. Maybe he didn't even want sex, maybe he just wanted to look, to imagine. Maybe he wanted a feeling of power, of being in control, of being the one to say, "You! You, how much?"

"It's kind of spooky out here, isn't it?" said Janis. "Makes me feel like I'm at the zoo."

"I know," I said. I was wondering what would happen if it were the johns who were arrested, exposed, humiliated — in the courts and the newspapers. What if people shrugged and said, "Well, obviously a woman needs to — but can you imagine a *man* who actually *buys* sex? He must be sick, a real case of arrested development. He must have had something terrible happen to him when he was young."

We were walking at a slower pace now, to my relief. We crossed and recrossed the street, looked into motel parking lots and alleys, stared down some of the drivers who slowed and honked at us.

"Creeps, perverts," Janis muttered.

I was staring at a car driving on the other side of the street. I could see a big man, hunched in a parka, staring at each woman. He reminded me of Art. It wasn't impossible.

"We could start asking some of the women," suggested Janis,

jogging in place to keep warm. "They'd probably recognize a new face."

"Get lost," the first girl we approached told us roughly. She was between fifteen and eighteen; her jeans were plastered to her legs and she was shivering in her low-cut blouse and thin nylon jacket.

Everyone told us the same thing. "Look, you're wrecking my business," a Black woman with a brassy helmet of hair said. "I don't know what your game is, but nobody's going to pick me up with you hanging around."

One threatened us with her pimp; another was too spaced out to understand what we were talking about. She nodded agreeably to everything we said and finally murmured, "That's a nice dog you have."

Finally we came to a woman who seemed to listen to us. She seemed older than most of the others, thickly made-up and wearing a curly auburn wig.

"No, I haven't seen her," she said. "But I'll watch out for her."

The motherly type, the good-hearted whore. It made me feel better, but Janis suddenly stiffened. "Oh god," she said. "You're an undercover cop, aren't you?"

The woman groaned. "Am I that obvious? I thought my make-up was great tonight."

"Are you here to arrest women?" I asked her.

"The men, actually. But I'm not getting many takers — too much competition from the kids. It's a good way of keeping an eye on the scene though. If I do see her, or if she gets picked up, you want me to give you a call?"

I was about to tell her yes, about to tell her that I thought the Portland police might have already gotten the word to look for her, but Janis nudged me sharply.

"No thanks," she said. "No need to get the police involved."

Walking away from the cop I remonstrated, "But they're already involved. I mean, Rosalie's dead and Trish might be next."

"Have you any idea what will happen if the cops pick her up for hooking?" Janis scolded me. "With her record and everything? She's a ward of the court in Washington; they could slap her in an institution so fast she wouldn't know what hit her and not let her out for years."

"You mean, all this time I've been thinking I was helping Trish by telling the police..."

"Let them solve Rosalie's murder," Janis said, "but keep Trish out of it if you can. The juvenile justice system is no joke."

We got back to Janis' before midnight, discouraged by what we'd seen.

"It's a different world out there," Janis admitted, going around to all the doors and windows and making sure they were locked. "All the prostitutes I've dealt with before were working out of their houses or escort services. The street scene's a hell of a lot rawer. . . It still doesn't make me change my mind about decriminalization," she hastened to assure me. "But, Jesus, what a life."

"I know," I said, slumping down on the couch. "It's so confusing though. How do you find out what your feelings about it really are? How do you say, No one should have to live this life — but if you want to, I support you — how do you judge without judging, anyway without sounding like an uptight wimp?"

Janis shook her head. "Be a hooker for a day? I'm afraid that's out for me. But what's funny is, when you think about it, this obsession feminism has with porn right now. These enormous battles fought around images and words and who has the right to use them or not. One side yelling *violence against women*, the other side shouting *censorship*. Nobody ever seems to ask the women who pose for the pictures and make the movies what they think. That's a lot harder to ignore when it comes to prostitution. The issue *is* the women. Which is probably why feminists don't take it up."

"Like they refused to take up lesbian issues until the lesbians themselves stood up and demanded to be recognized?"

"Exactly."

She made up the sofa bed for me and we said good-night. I undressed and got under the covers, took out the diary Trish's father had given me and began to read.

32

SEPTEMBER 1. Ever since Julianne talked about her Dad I have been remembering a lot of things. Really far back things, that happened when I was little. I don't even know how old, or if they started to happen earlier, before I was old enough to remember. Somehow I have this memory, kind of like a dream, where it's dark in my room, with a little crack of light coming under the door. Then there isn't any light anymore. My Dad comes in, somehow it's too quiet and he's too big. He hugs me, but somehow it's not nice, it's strange and scary. He keeps hugging me too tight and breathing too hard. It's really dark and he tells me not to say anything.

"Another time, I'm in the bathtub and he tells my Mom he's going to wash me. He plays a game with me under the soap bubbles and I'm laughing and screaming because he's tickling me. Then he says he's going to make pee-pee and not to tell Mommy. I feel like there's something wrong, but I don't know what.

"Whenever I think of my Dad when I'm little, it's like there's this feeling attached to it. A kind of scared feeling, like he's too big and I feel smothered. It's like when you're having a bad dream and you want to scream, but you open your mouth and nothing comes out and you don't know if it's because you're in a dream and can't make a noise, or if it's real and you've lost your voice.

"Mom and Dad got divorced when I was six. I don't even remember anything about it. He was gone one day and Mom said he wasn't coming back. She was really nice to me for a long time. I guess I felt sad that he was gone, but I must have been relieved too, because nobody came into my room at night.

"I must have forgotten about him and everything, because I remember when I was ten and Mom said, You're going to Portland to visit your Dad and his wife and new baby, I was really happy. I can't remember having any weird feelings about him. No wait, I remember I didn't like to be alone with him. And sometimes I had bad dreams when I was at their house, like I had this feeling something was pressing down on me. But when I woke up, nothing was.

"*September 4.* I almost said something in the group tonight about my Dad, but then I didn't feel like it. I was going to call up Mom and ask her why they got divorced, but I didn't do that either. She gets so upset when I talk to her, and Rob would be there and he probably wouldn't even let me talk to her anyway. Today at the center I met two girls, Rosalie and Karen. They just stopped by to check it out, they just came to Seattle. Karen is on the streets. Rosalie isn't. She's the first person I met who stopped because she didn't want to anymore. She said one day she just couldn't anymore, it made her sick. I don't do it much anymore but there's no other way to get money.

"*September 6.* Got high with Rosalie and Karen in their room. The thing I hate about living in the group house is that I don't have any privacy. And we're not supposed to get high either. It was good getting high, it made me forget about my Dad. Rosalie said she's going to be a dealer, that's the only way if you don't date. I told her about Wayne, but I said I didn't feel like seeing him. Karl got him started but now Wayne does all the business. I feel sorry for Karl sometimes but he sort of gives me the creeps how he lives so I don't want to see him either.

"*September 8.* Whenever I'm not high, I think about my Dad. I keep feeling really mad. At least Wayne treated me like a real person, I mean, he told me what we were doing and explained it and everything. And he loved me, so it was all right. My Dad just did it to me when I was a little kid, when I didn't understand. It's really scary thinking about being so little, only five years old, and having that happen.

"*September 15.* Rosalie is down because Karen split. Karen said she was sick of supporting her because Rosalie wouldn't do dates, but Rosalie said she was still going to deal drugs if she could, she didn't want to do it with a man again. She couldn't. Now she just wants to get high all the time. I've been doing it a lot too, because I know if I didn't I might go down to Portland and confront my Dad. I guess the reason I don't is I'm afraid he'd say he didn't do anything. He's such a hypocrite, talking about Jesus all the time and going to church. Rosalie keeps bugging me about Wayne and getting some coke from him. I said if we hooked up with him again we'd have to do dates all the time, just like I did before. She said she wouldn't work for no white pimp and I'd be a fool if I did too. But I said she didn't know Wayne, how he was. He wasn't ever mean, he just talked you into things, and then there was this weird way you felt like you belonged to him. It's harder now taking care of myself than it was with him. She said she still wanted to get some coke from him. She said, be tough girl, she said I could depend on her. But she doesn't know Wayne, how he makes you feel.

"Yesterday I didn't go back to the group house, I think it's fucked they have this curfew. I didn't go to the center either, to the group, because I did some dates last night and don't feel like telling them. It doesn't do any good anyway. I used to think talking made me feel better about myself, but now I don't think anything can."

That was the last diary entry. Trish had come down to Portland and her father had lied to her, just as she thought he would. After that, nothing much had mattered anymore. She had started working for Wayne again, taking drugs, maybe supporting

Rosalie. Had Rosalie gone back to prostitution herself, or had she managed to become a dealer? Had she worked with Wayne, or against him? And how did Karl, the man who gave Trish the creeps, fit into all this?

The diary didn't give me the answers I wanted. I looked through it again. In the back was a folded torn piece of paper tucked into the pages.

"Dear Art,

I know what you did, even if you say you didn't. I don't care if you say you didn't. I hate you, you are not my father. You hurt me when I couldn't do anything about it and real fathers don't do that to their kids. I will never forgive you first because you did what you did and second because you lied to me. I will hate you til the day I die.

Patricia."

33

P ORTLANDIA AND SISTERS OF THE ROAD were not the only models of help in the city; every agency had its own perspective on the problem of street kids, why they were there and what to do about it. I called the numbers Beth had given me and met with everyone she'd suggested.

It was a long Monday.

The social workers seemed uniformly optimistic in their jargon. They talked about social service delivery systems and quoted statistics to show how their various programs were succeeding. They talked about broken homes, sexual abuse, families that were no longer "intact," drug and alcohol problems, as if such things could be solved by a little peer group interaction, a job counselor, a case worker's timely intervention. They talked about the rapport they had with kids and how there was no problem getting kids to talk, to confide, to trust them.

But the man at the drop-in center had a much bleaker view.

"Kids tell social workers and cops what they want to hear. It's not really manipulative, not intentionally, it's just a way of getting adults off their backs. Most adults feel a need to solve a kid's problems. That's what they're trained to do and what they feel comfortable doing. But it's really a form of control. What the kids need is a safe space just to talk, an outlet for what happens to them on the streets. I don't try to intervene unless they ask for help. I only ask two things of them: that they stay alive and that they not pass on the abuse."

His name was Joe and he looked an overgrown kid himself, a tall, weedy man wearing jeans, a white shirt with rolled-up sleeves and suspenders. I couldn't quite fit him into any of the categories I had for people in the helping professions. He refused to keep his distance; what was going on out in the streets pained him as if it were happening to his own children, or himself. Even Beth, who cared so much, seemed far more self-protective.

Most of the social workers I'd talked to seemed to take my search for Trish for granted, or else they never asked. But Joe pushed me. "Why are you looking, what's it to you?"

How easy if I could have said, "I'm a private eye," or "I'm a cop." How easy if I could have hid behind some professional label, instead of having to admit I had no claim on her, was in no one's service. I couldn't even say I knew her very well, or that by finding her I'd be able to do anything to change her life. Maybe it was my own life I wanted to change.

"I just need to find her, that's all."

Joe looked at me. All around there were kids, kids talking, laughing, trying on clothes from the free racks, helping themselves to toothpaste and soap from the free boxes, even sleeping amidst all the noise. In one corner was a girl crying and a boy attempting to comfort her; in another was a group playing cards. None of them looked more than sixteen.

"Don't feel so sorry for them," Joe said. "There's a lot to admire and learn from here. Kids who leave home for the streets have a lot of courage. They could have stayed and taken the abuse at home. They didn't. The way to support them is to tap into that courage."

"But how do you get them to trust you?" I asked. "What does it take?"

"Only one thing," he said, and laughed a little. "The hardest thing of all. You've got to be trustworthy."

*

By the time I got home I was exhausted and fully conscious that I'd gotten nowhere. Janis had told me I was on my own for dinner; she was working late. I heated up some Szechuwan Tofu Triangles and had a beer. Then I called Detective Logan.

He was working late and his voice was flat with an undertone of frustration.

"We found Wayne. Talked to him briefly. He wouldn't say more than that your friend Trish was his stepsister. He had no idea where she was and he didn't know a Rosalie or an Abby."

"That's a lie!"

"Prosecuting a pimp is almost impossible. Even with testimony. Building a drug case or a murder case takes a lot of investigation. Wayne may be everything you say he is, but it's going to take time and hard work to prove it. And I don't have enough men as it is."

"But he had Rosalie's fake ID! Doesn't that prove anything?"

"Maybe, maybe not. For now we'll keep an eye on him, and if you find out anything more, give me a call."

Like when I find Trish's murdered body somewhere?

"What about Karl?" I said.

"He wasn't at the address you gave us. We'll keep trying."

Fucking police, I thought helplessly as I hung up. Am I supposed to do everything on my own?

I was still sitting by the phone when it rang.

"Hello, hello? I want to talk to Pam Nilsen. Is this Pam?" She was shouting as if she were calling from Singapore. The connection was clear as a bell.

"Hi Carole."

"Pam, I feel like we had a misunderstanding the other night. I never dreamed you'd leave town because of it."

"I didn't. I'm here to look for Trish."

"It's not that I don't think you're attractive. You're a very attractive woman. It's just that you took me by surprise."

"It's all right, Carole. It wouldn't have worked out."

She was still shouting. "But I've been thinking about it. Why the hell not? Live dangerously. Screw the rules. Take a chance. I think I'll come down and join you."

"No, don't do that," I said, horrified. "I mean, I like you, it's not that, but I'm pretty busy here. Look, can't we just forget the whole thing? I made a mistake, I got carried away for a moment, it was just . . . just the coke."

"You made a mistake?" she shouted. Then her voice suddenly dropped. "Oh, all right. I just thought I'd give you a second chance."

"Well, I appreciate it, Carole. Maybe some other time . . ."

"Yeah!" she said cheerfully. "Maybe sometime when you're not working at Best."

Now what the hell did that mean? I wondered as I hung up. Were she and June planning a coup? Still, I felt better. It was nice of Carole to give me a chance to reject her too. Now we were even, which is more than you could say of most relationships, embryonic, full-fledged or over.

I had another beer and looked through Janis' books, decided they were too hard for me, and turned on the TV to watch *Cagney and Lacey*.

Detective Lacey was pregnant and at home. Her husband Harve, the one good man in the world, was his usual loving and nurturing self. Sergeant Cagney, meanwhile, was following a rape case, helped by an overeager young woman officer who stayed up all night feeding data into the computer. Why was this young woman so determined to find the rapist, to the detriment of her own career and the good name of the 14th Precinct? "I'm sure he's the man we're looking for!" "Until we've got proof, we can't do anything," Cagney said, uncharacteristically cautious. She looked through the medical files of the young woman officer and found that she had once been a rape victim. Ah-hah. A personal vendetta. She hadn't been able to find her rapist, so she'd fixated on this one.

They gave the officer a medical leave, but she secretly kept on the case. She rented a room in the area where the rapist had attacked his victims and she donned a long brown wig — all his victims had long brown hair. There was a horrifying scene of her waiting in the rented room at night, propped up on the pillows like a child, the window open, the curtains blowing eerily in the wind. Cagney found out at the last minute where she was and raced to the scene, only to find that there had been a homicide, and the room was filled with cops. She had killed the rapist.

The young woman officer had sacrificed her police future to get revenge, not on the man who'd raped her, but on the man who'd raped so many others. She had taken the law into her own hands because the law didn't protect women.

She and Cagney looked at each other and the scene froze, the series' trademark ending.

And I almost burst into tears. It was as if I understood the story on some profound level and was afraid of its meaning. Was that the only way to stop violence against women? To kill men? To kill them back?

I didn't want to believe that.

Janis came in like a quiet cyclone. "What? Watching television? I thought you'd be out on the streets still."

"I'm exhausted," I said. What I meant was, I couldn't face it, couldn't face the eyes of the men in the cars.

"I hear you," she said unexpectedly. "I'm beat too." She collapsed next to me on the couch. "I notice that whenever I don't have a lover I work like a maniac. I just hate those evenings home alone."

"Yeah."

We sat for a moment, almost companionably, missing people, then I asked her, "Was it hard for you? Breaking up with Beth?"

"Oh, I knew it was coming, it couldn't last. She'd just close down when I tried to talk to her; that's her way, she shuts down, she can't help it. Which just makes me more anxious, more demanding, I guess. Vicious circle."

She brushed her hair behind her ears and leaned her head back, but when the phone rang she leapt up to answer it. I had the feeling she was always waiting for a call. I'd been like that myself last summer.

"It's for you," she said. "A man."

Art didn't even say hello. "I've found her, I've found Patti," he roared. "Safe and sound."

"Where was she?"

"Oh, I just drove past her and recognized her by chance. Since you told me she might be in Portland I've kept my eyes peeled."

Just drove by? I wondered if he *had* been out on Sandy Boulevard. "That's great," I said. "Can I talk to her?"

"Just for a minute." He seemed reluctant. "She's tired. But she's all right."

Trish came on the line. "Pam?"

"Hi," I said. "I've been worried about you."

She was silent.

"Is it hard to talk because your father's there? I'll come and see you tomorrow."

"Pam," she said again. This time it wasn't a question, but a flat little hopeless bleat.

Art took the phone. "Safe and sound," he said. "No need for you to worry. I'll take care of her now."

"I'm coming to see her tomorrow."

"Well, maybe," he said. "We'll have to see how she's feeling. Judy wants to take her shopping you know."

"I'll call you in the morning."

"We'll have to see," he said and hung up quickly. I had a feeling he was sorry he'd told me anything about his relationship with Trish. Now he was asserting his parental rights. But did he have any?

"Well, she's not dead and not in the detention center," Janis said pragmatically when I told her. "That's the important thing."

"No, she's safe," I said. "Now all we have to do is get her away from her father."

34

T HE NEXT MORNING I CALLED ART. "She's still sleeping."

At ten they were "eating breakfast." And at ten thirty there was no answer. Shopping perhaps. But what if they were shopping all day? What if when they came home they were "eating dinner"? I was never going to get to talk with Trish, to ask her all the things I wanted to know.

I called Beth at home to ask for her help. If she came to Portland she could say she was Trish's social worker, and Art would have to let us see her.

"I don't have any real authority," Beth demurred.

"But he doesn't know that. We could even take her with us back to Seattle."

"Let's not get carried away...Remember, she may be safer there with him watching her every move than back in Seattle. Maybe she should just stay there until everything's cleared up."

I realized Beth didn't know about the incest. "She's not going to stay there. She'll run."

Beth thought about it a minute. "Maybe you're right. Okay, I'll come. I should get there about three or so."

I thought about surprising Janis, but decided it wouldn't be fair. It was bad enough that I found myself nourishing a few gentle desires in Beth's direction. So I called Janis' office and told her that Beth was coming and why.

Her crisp assurance took on a tone of uncertainty. "Don't let her leave again before I get home," she said. "I'll try to be back by six at the latest. Don't let her leave. I'll make dinner... I'll make a meat dish. And tell her," Janis thought quickly, "tell her she can smoke in my house."

Beth arrived at two-thirty, wearing a heavy, unfashionable coat and a soft pink angora hat that rode her strawberry hair like a dab of fruit mousse. There was something grand and commanding about her in motion, even though she seemed entirely unconscious of it. She held her car keys tightly in her fingers like a baby holding a rattle.

It felt good to see her, but it didn't feel anything like love; it didn't make me tense up and stop breathing as Janis had done on the phone. Even when Beth hugged me I didn't feel much of anything but relief. It was a little disappointing.

"Did you manage to get a hold of them on the phone?" she asked, while looking around Janis' living room in a thoughtful, remembering kind of way.

"Finally—just five minutes ago. I told him we were coming over. There wasn't much he could say."

Beth nodded, still absorbed in some private memory. "I'm just glad she's safe," she said finally.

"I guess she's safe..." I told her about Trish's diary and Art's confession.

"Christ!" she said. "I remember Julianne and all that incest stuff last summer in the group. A couple of other girls started talking about it too. But I never thought...Trish..." she sighed, a little grimly. "Well, what is it you want me to do?"

"Keep him occupied talking about whatever social workers talk about—custody and placement, whatever—while I ask Trish some questions."

"Professional jargon, in other words." She started to light a Carlton, then stopped.

"It's all right. Janis told me you could smoke in the house."

164

"Did she?" was all Beth said.

Art was waiting for us in the living room with Trish. Judy had taken the kids to the playground. He was obsequious and eager to please; he kept wetting his big, grayish-pink lips as he told us how he'd taken the day off from his job at the hospital (he was in payroll, been there for eight years) and how they'd gone shopping and had lunch at Burger King and tonight they were going to go to see a movie, the whole family.

Trish seemed younger than when I'd seen her last. She wore no makeup and her hair was washed and bouncy on her shoulders. Instead of her tight jeans and white leather jacket she had on a skirt and a blouse with a Peter Pan collar. She looked entirely defeated and didn't seem to want to meet my eyes.

"Remember me?" I tried to joke.

"Yeah," she said sullenly and stared at her shoes; they were new too — low pumps with bows. Judy's idea of teen fashion.

For the first time it struck me that I knew Trish much better than she knew me. Ever since she'd left my apartment I'd done little but follow her. I'd met her parents, Wayne, Karl, her street friends, Beth. I'd read her diary and snooped into the hotel room she'd shared with Rosalie. I'd told the police about her and I'd told Art she was in Portland. And suddenly I wasn't sure how I could justify any of this, much less use it now.

If you want them to trust you, be trustworthy, Joe at the drop-in center had told me. That wasn't going to be easy.

Beth took control immediately. She hugged Trish and said matter-of-factly, "Glad to see you girl. Glad you're all right." Then she turned to Art, authoritative in her big coat. "Is there someplace we can speak privately?"

He hesitated and looked at Trish and me. "The kitchen, I guess."

When they were gone I said quickly, "I did tell your father you were in Portland, Trish. I'm sorry. I've been looking for you for a week and I've been — so frightened that something had happened to you."

"Nothing has happened to me," she muttered.

"Why did you leave my apartment, did someone take you here?"

"I just felt like leaving, I just felt like getting out of Seattle." For the first time she raised her head and her expression was challenging. "It's a free country, isn't it?"

"Look," I said a little desperately. "I've met Wayne. I know about you and Wayne and Rosalie. I know about Karl. Was it one of them, Wayne or Karl, who brought you here?"

Something flickered in her eyes. Fear? Or anger?

"I don't want to talk about Wayne with you. You wouldn't understand."

"I would!"

She was stubbornly silent. I heard voices in the kitchen: Art's eager explanations, Beth's noncommittal reassurances. I wondered what she was telling him.

"Why don't you want to talk about Wayne?" I persisted, in what I hoped was a calmer tone. "Are you afraid of him, afraid he'll hurt you if you say anything?"

Again that strange flicker in her eyes. But she said obstinately, "Wayne wouldn't hurt me. He loves me."

She wanted to believe it still. "If he loves you so much why didn't he want you to stop being a prostitute? Rosalie got out of the life, didn't she? And she wanted you to stop too. Is that what made Wayne mad?"

"Rosalie," she said. She closed her eyes. "Just leave me alone, will you?"

"Why did Wayne have Rosalie's fake ID? And why is Wayne afraid of Karl?" I heard the voices in the kitchen pause, as if they'd come to some agreement. "I'm only trying to help you, Trish."

"Oh sure," she said. "Big help, telling Art you thought I was in Portland. How do you think I felt when some guy stopped and I got in and saw it was my fucking father?" She stared at me with eyes full of hate and desperation. "Well, I'm not staying here, if that's what any of you think. And you and Beth can go fuck yourselves. I'm not telling you anything. There's nothing to tell anyway."

I couldn't let it go. "What about Rob? It couldn't have been him, could it?"

"Rob?" She gritted her teeth like an animal at bay. "You've been talking to *him* too? Jesus Christ."

Art and Beth came back into the living room in time for Art to hear her take his savior's name in vain. He flinched and then said heartily, "Well, have you two been having a nice talk?"

Beth looked from Trish to me, saying gently, "I think it's best if you stay here for a day or two longer, Trish. We'll get things straightened out as soon as we can."

Trish didn't bother to look at her.

Art came over and patted his daughter clumsily on the shoulder. She stiffened but he ignored it. "I was thinking that before the movie maybe we should all go out to dinner tonight, Patti. You and me and Judy and the kids. You like fish and chips I seem to remember."

"I want to go with Beth and Pam." She suddenly panicked and lunged away from him, towards us.

I wanted to grab her and make a run for it, and afterwards I wished I had. "I'll call you," I said instead. "I'll come visit you tomorrow."

"Don't bother," she said.

35

BETH AND I RETURNED to Janis' to wait for her. It was good to be inside. The bright cold weather had snapped, and a windy rainstorm swirled over the city like an upside-down Jacuzzi.

"It's strange to be here again," said Beth, reclining on the couch with her pink bedroom slippers up. "I spent so many weekends here during the fall." She pulled out her Carltons and lit one, sucking greedily. "This is the first time Janis ever let me smoke in her house." But she didn't look particularly pleased. I was beginning to realize that underneath Beth's calm exterior she was just as tightly wound up as Janis, perhaps even more so, for Janis at least expelled her nervous energy in activity and Beth didn't move a muscle she didn't have to.

I told her that Trish hadn't given me any answers, but that I still had hopes I might get something out of her tomorrow. "If I can just make her trust me."

Beth shook her head. "I feel pretty shitty leaving her with her father, even though I can't think quite what else to do at the moment. At some point I'm going to have to make a report or tell somebody and then it's going to be the same old legal rigamarole.

A group home may not want her with her history of running and I hate to turn her back to the foster care system. But I'll have to do something. Her father doesn't have a legal right to keep her. Her mother had custody and gave it up to the state. He wants to get her back, he says, but if she doesn't want to stay with him, and obviously she doesn't, he'll probably lose. I wish to hell she was eighteen, I wish she knew what the fuck she was doing with her life. . . And I still can't believe I never suspected she was an incest survivor. It makes me wonder why I'm in counseling at all, if I can be that blind."

"Why are you? In counseling, I mean."

"As opposed to what—in the legal profession?" Beth smiled tiredly, rubbing her freckled temples. "Don't you know the counseling profession is full of people like me? People who've been there—as incest survivors, addicts, battered wives, you name it—and want to help. Plenty of times I've wondered if that's healthy. I mean, look at me." She pointed to her fluffy pink slippers. "Am I a good role model? But I was down and out myself and I understand what the street's about. Though I've sometimes wondered if social work is just a way of staying in contact with what I know best and the crowd of people I know best."

"Was that a problem, with you and Janis?"

Beth thought about it. "Of course that was part of it. But there were other things. For all her organization and decided opinions Janis is a pretty open person. She doesn't dream of hiding herself from a person she's close to. And I do. Sometimes I tell people I was an unwed mother, sometimes I say I'm a recovering alcoholic, but when I've said that I usually don't say any more. I can open up once in a while to kids, strangely enough, but not really to lovers—not really to anyone at all."

She lit another Carlton and didn't meet my eyes. "It would take—I don't know what it would take—to make me open up. And that's what Janis wanted, that's what she expected. Frankly, I was terrified."

"But she still loves you."

"She loves the person she thinks I am. Not the real Beth. Nobody could ever love the real Beth." She heard herself and laughed, rather glumly. "See why I make such a good counselor? My issues are the same."

I didn't think Janis had made a mistake. I thought she was right in reaching out to the qualities Beth had in such abundance —strength, good humor, generosity, solidity—even if Beth couldn't always see them herself. But I didn't say anything more. I was opposed to matchmaking, especially the second time around. Besides, I was attracted to Beth myself.

"What about you?" she asked.

I told her about Hadley. How she'd loved and left me. "She said she was a rescuer and I didn't need her help."

"And you just let that go? You didn't think that maybe she was finally doing something good for herself by choosing you?"

I was dumbfounded. It rarely occurred to me to challenge Hadley's perception of herself or me. "I suppose," I said slowly, "I can pursue someone a little bit in the beginning and I can say no to people who pursue me, but I never feel I can change someone's mind about me. I guess I usually feel that they know what they want and I just have to accept it."

"Sometimes that's sensible, sometimes that's too passive." I could see Beth felt more comfortable in the role of advisor. She leaned forward with a therapeutic look in her eye. "What would happen if you went to Houston? You came to Portland, after all. What would happen if you said—like you as much said to Trish, 'I can't forget you, Hadley. I won't let you go so easily.'?"

"I'd feel like I was in a bad movie."

"But you could write her or call her, couldn't you? Find out how she's doing, keep in touch?"

"Yes . . ." I felt the conversation was going the wrong way and tried to steer it back. "Are you involved with anyone new?"

Beth didn't pick up on my hint. "I'm giving myself a rest for awhile. Janis was plenty."

In spite of her urging me to pursue Hadley and not take no for an answer, I didn't think Beth would respond if I tried the same approach on her. Or it may have been that underneath I didn't think she was really finished with Janis. I didn't think they were finished with each other.

Janis rushed in at six, precisely as promised, with two big bags of groceries. Even knowing her as little as I did, I could tell she was in an anxious state of euphoria.

"I'm going to make Veal Florentine," she announced. "And eggplant."

"Do you need any help?" I asked.

"No, no." She was all efficiency, brushing her hair behind her ears, mentally putting on an apron. She had hardly looked at Beth.

"Don't be silly, of course you do. We'll pound the veal or something—I know vegetarians have tender sensibilities—and we'll keep you company." Beth lowered her pink slippers to the floor and shuffled after her into the kitchen. "We promise not to get involved with the sauce."

"That'd be . . . that'd be nice then," Janis said. "I mean about the veal. I mean—I'd like the company."

That night at dinner I watched Janis and Beth maneuver around and towards each other. At first it seemed hopeless—when Janis would open up and reveal something, Beth would automatically withdraw. Then Janis would go quiet and Beth would worry and try to make up for it by drawing Janis out. Then the whole cycle would begin again.

In between we ate Janis' delicious dinner and made small talk about innocent subjects, like Central America and Reaganomics, issues we could all agree on.

I thought it was going to be a long evening but gradually, almost imperceptibly, it began to get better. More laughter, more enthusiasm, more honesty. The two of them stopped trying so hard, stopped worrying about offending each other and started to enjoy themselves.

I enjoyed myself too, when I wasn't thinking about Trish, or, increasingly, about Hadley. *Had* I given up too easily? *Was* it useless? I thought of her long legs and plain face, her Texas twang and turquoise eyes, and a remembrance of her sweetness came over me so strongly that I could have almost eaten it instead of the cheesecake for dessert.

Eventually I became so preoccupied that I forgot to pay attention to Janis and Beth and it was a slight shock to me when I came to and heard them discussing Trish.

"You can't tell me she's in love with that pimp of hers," Janis was saying, leaning forward with her elbows on the table. "That's not love, it's emotional slavery."

"I've been in love like that," said Beth. "It's not healthy, but it is love."

"With whom?" Janis demanded.

"With—a guy—once." Beth shut up and then the words came bursting out, brokenly, "You wouldn't understand that kind of masochistic—self-destructive—behavior."

"Why don't you let me try? Why the fuck won't you ever let me try?" Janis said, standing up.

Beth stood up too, then started stacking the dishes and moving towards the kitchen.

"You're *not* planning to drive back to Seattle now, are you?" Janis panicked and ran after her.

Beth looked at her, opened her mouth and then closed it again and shook her head.

The emotional tension in the air made its own electrical field. I was afraid that if I stood up too I'd be electrocuted.

They slept together that night. I know, I heard them.

And I can tell you, it made me feel as lonely as hell.

172

36

W<small>HEN</small> I <small>WOKE UP</small> the next morning Beth was already gone and
Janis was halfway out the door. Dressed in a gray tweed pants
suit with a blue striped cravat at her neck, she was her professional, efficient self, and betrayed no signs of passion.

"I'll come by for you at two this afternoon. We'll go visit Trish,"
she threw over her shoulder crisply, adding, "You can tell Art I'm
her lawyer if he makes any fuss."

I lay on my back for a while and the terrier came over and
licked my hand. She stared at me in a woefully friendly way that
made me long for Ernesto's indifference.

It's worth a try, I thought, and before I could wake up enough
to decide I was doing the wrong thing, I got the Houston operator
to give me Hadley's father's phone number.

"Hi, it's Pam."

"Pam! Pam!" she gulped and burst out happily, "It's great to
hear your voice."

I saw her so vividly that for a moment I could hardly speak.
Then I managed to get a few sentences out. "I just wanted
to check out your Texas accent. How're you doing? How's

your dad?"

"Oh—the same, pretty much. He doesn't drink anymore, that's the only good thing. One half his body's paralyzed and he can barely talk. Still his charming self though. How are you—what's happening?"

Before I knew it I was telling her about Trish and Rosalie, the murder and the search. It felt good to talk; but somehow it only made me miss her more. She should have been with me through all this.

"You don't just sit around, do you?" she whistled. "And all this time I've just been imagining you at the print shop, churning out the latest political poster."

"You do think about me sometimes then?"

She paused. "I think about you a lot. I like you, Pam."

"You said you liked me when you walked away, too."

"I know...I've often thought of that. But I felt I had to do it at the time. It was all so quick...and you scared me somehow. I thought I'd disappoint you."

"Disappoint me—how?"

"I thought that when you really got to know me...well, it's silly, isn't it? I wasn't very happy without you when it came down to it. Have you missed me?"

I thought of my loneliness at living alone, my brief affairs and failures to connect. I thought of meeting Trish and how that had changed me, had made me start caring again for somebody besides myself.

"I wouldn't go through it again. But I've learned a lot. Nothing like what I expected when I became a lesbian. I thought it was going to be like one of those lesbian Harlequin romances. A little confusion and then the happy ending, souls and bodies merging into Sapphic oneness. We had the happy ending first, then the confusion."

She laughed and I could almost see the way one side of her mouth turned up, the way her turquoise eyes closed. "I'm planning to come back to Seattle in February. What do you think? Are you going to be around?"

"Yes," I said. "Very much around."

The day picked up after that. I made myself some breakfast,

took the dog for a walk and found it in my heart to wish Beth and Janis well.

Then I called Detective Logan again. No, he wasn't there. No, she didn't know if he'd talked to Karl yet. Yes, they had my number in Portland. Yes, he'd call me if anything came up.

I tried to tell myself that the police had it under control and that I shouldn't worry. Logan would probably get more out of Wayne or Karl than I could, if they were in Seattle. And if they weren't? If one of them was in Portland looking for Trish? I tried not to think about it, nor what would happen if I were all wrong and it was somebody else, somebody like Rob for instance, looking for her.

I decided to call the Hemmings' house just to reassure myself. No answer. From the hosiery department Melanie told me that Rob was out looking for work today. He wouldn't be back until late.

"Why?" she asked.

Because I think your husband is a murderer? It was impossible, I couldn't tell her that.

"I just wanted to ask him something," I said evasively. Then I told her I was in Portland and that Trish was at her father's.

"Oh," she said, struggling not to care.

"...I know about what happened when she was young, Melanie. And so does Trish."

"I blame myself," she said finally. "I never told her about her father. I didn't think she'd remember. And he's changed. He's different now, I guess. But I should have told her. I just didn't know how."

It was the first time I'd heard Melanie take any responsibility for what had happened to Trish and it gave me a little hope.

In fact, I was feeling quite hopeful when I put down the phone. I started thinking about Hadley again and about Trish when this was all over. Maybe she could work part-time at Best Printing. I wouldn't push her to go back to school, but I'd give her books to read. Beth had said it could take years to get off the streets, but I'd help her find a way. I wouldn't even care if she didn't become a radical feminist.

Janis called and broke into my happy reverie.

"Something's come up and I can't make it when I said I would. Can we do it this evening instead? I'd really like to go with you.

175

To—ah—get to know Trish."

A strange feeling told me it was better not to wait, that I should go over there myself. But I didn't want to disappoint Janis; she was probably trying to show Beth that she could spare a little time for one of her charges.

"Sure. I'll just call to make sure she's all right."

Trish was taking a nap, said Judy Margolin with disapproval in her voice. "She's been sleeping practically all the time since she got here."

"Well, she's probably tired."

"I suppose so."

"Has she made any phone calls?"

"Not as far as I know. There's a phone upstairs, but like I said, she's been sleeping."

"We'll be over at seven or so then."

It was still raining, but I was restless and took the dog out again. I walked over to the Margolin's house and looked at it. That odd little twinge hadn't gone away. Somehow I felt worried about Trish and what she might do. I wondered if having a lawyer around would make Trish any more willing to tell me what she knew.

The house looked cozy in the heavy rain, but the wind chimes clattered with an eerie sound. I told myself that I was just being stupid and went back to Janis'.

Janis arrived home late, after seven, and seemed frustratingly preoccupied. I'd spent a slow afternoon reading and longing for the print shop. June might not believe me, but this self-imposed vacation was getting on my nerves.

When we finally pulled up in front of the Margolin's house, we found a scene of confusion. Art was wandering around on the porch with a flashlight. He was wearing an enormous yellow slicker that made him look like a large warning light. He was calling in a loud, anxious voice, "Patricia, Patti!" Judy was standing in the doorway with one of the children in her arms; the other held on to her dress with a scared expression.

"Dammit," said Janis. "Now we'll have to go looking for her all over again. This could get tedious."

I walked up to the porch and asked Art, "When did she leave?"

"She was sleeping while we ate dinner. We decided not to wake her. But when I went up afterwards she was gone. Patricia!" he called helplessly, as if she were a kitten who'd strayed. "Where are you?"

A porch light next door went on and an elderly woman in a housecoat came out. "Art, is that you? What's going on?"

"My daughter's run away," he wailed through the rain. "My fifteen-year-old daughter from Seattle. Have you seen her?"

The woman didn't hesitate. "Twenty minutes ago I saw a car pull up and someone from your house run out and get into it."

My heart skidded like an ice cube in my chest. "Did you see who was driving? Was it a man?"

"It was definitely a man," she said.

"Old or young. Was he bald?"

She considered. "Older, I think. And he was wearing a sort of cap. I noticed the license plate though. I always notice the license plate because you can't be too careful these days. It was from Washington State."

I was just in time to catch the eight o'clock train.

177

37

I GOT INTO SEATTLE LATE and didn't sleep well, kept having dreams that someone was driving me somewhere down an unlit country road at night. Sometimes I was in the back seat and there was blood everywhere; sometimes I was in the passenger's seat and couldn't see the driver. How did I get here? I kept wondering, in that terrified, frantic way you do in dreams. Did I get in on my own? Where are we going, what's going to happen to me? Is it my fault this is happening?

In the morning I called Detective Logan, the first act of what was to be a long, frustrating day.

Detective Logan wanted to know why I hadn't told him about meeting Trish in Portland and why I hadn't called the police there. Because I thought I could handle it myself was not the right answer. After we'd discussed my attitude, he grudgingly told me that they'd been watching Wayne and hadn't seen him go anywhere. They were trying to get a search warrant. As for Karl, he seemed to have vanished completely.

I decided to do a little more investigating on my own, in spite of Logan's admonitions to "just leave it to us now." Art's next door neighbor had said the man who picked up Trish was older. I couldn't imagine her calling Rob or willingly going with him, so it must have been Karl she chose to rescue her. Or Karl who had come anyway.

I went back to his studio around noon. There was no answer to my knock and the door was firmly locked. Taking a chance, I tried a few other doors down the hall. Eventually I heard a "Yeah, come on in."

The studio I entered was the complete opposite of Karl's: bright white and modern with a varnished wood floor and pale light streaming in through the tiny-paned windows. The man inside was standing near the windows, with a long pipe in his hands. On one end of the pipe was a bubble of blue glass and he was spinning it rapidly over a flame. As I watched, the blue sphere flattened and became a disk. He laid it aside and turned to me.

"What can I do for you?"

"I wonder if you know an artist named Karl Devize?"

He was a young man in jeans and a plaid shirt, cheerful and unremarkable. But his open, friendly face shut down when I mentioned Karl's name.

"Are you from the Health Department or the police?" he asked, carefully turning down the flame.

"Well—neither. I'm just looking for a girl and I think Karl might know where she is."

"The last time I saw Karl, he was drunk out of his mind, puking in the hallway," the young man said. "I'd be surprised if he answered his door these days. We've been trying to get him out of the building for the past three months. He's supposed to be evicted next week. That's probably why he's not around."

"So you wouldn't have noticed if he'd been gone last night, would you?"

"No, I make a point not to notice what he's up to. It's usually too disgusting. When he first moved in he was pretty obnoxious, but he was interesting at least. Now he's just sloppy."

"What changed him?"

"Drugs and drink, simple as that. I gather he was dealing drugs for a while. I don't know if he does now. I can't imagine he's together enough for that."

"Did you ever see a couple of young girls hanging around here, a Black girl and a white girl, about fifteen?"

The man snorted. "Not exactly. He's a faggot, for one thing. There used to be young boys sometimes, you'd meet them in the hall. But now I think he's just in love with alcohol."

"What about a guy named Wayne? Wayne Hemmings? Is he gay too?"

"Who knows?" He shrugged. "I think he was one of Karl's protégés at first, but it's hard to tell. You see them around together a lot, but I'm not sure if Wayne feels sorry for Karl or if he really gets a kick out of the guy.

"It's not that Wayne is an especially good artist," the man went on. "I don't know how he survives—probably dealing drugs—but he seems too smart to be hanging around with someone like Karl."

He picked up his long pipe again and put it to his lips. I took that as a sign that he'd told me all he knew. I thanked him and left.

I tried Wayne's apartment at the Redmond twice that day, but he either wasn't around or wasn't answering his door. It made me wonder how the cops could be so sure he was still in Seattle.

That night June, Carole and I had dinner at my place. It was partly to make up for my absence and partly in honor of a letter from Penny, brought back from Nicaragua by a friend. June had received it while I was in Portland and suggested we all read it together.

Carole arrived first. I expected a little mutual embarrassment, but she was breezy and bouncy as ever, more so because she'd managed to find a new lover in the last couple of days.

"She's incredibly interesting, Pam," Carole assured me, perched on a stool in the kitchen and shredding lettuce with dreamy abandon. "She's been all over the world, like to Nepal and stuff. She tells these wonderful stories about trekking and sherpas and everything. I'm so *envious*."

"Wait a minute. Not Devlin?"

"Oh, that's right, she said she knew you slightly."

Slightly.

"*Another* girlfriend?" June said when she heard, then remembered her manners. "Well, congratulations. I hope you'll be very happy together." ›

"Oh, I think so," said Carole eagerly. "Sometimes you just

180

know, like practically in the first instant, if someone's going to be right for you. Maybe that's romantic, but I don't care. We've already got a lot of plans—we're going to go traveling together. Bali, I guess." She made some Balinese hand movements to illustrate. "It's a very artistic culture there. I know I'll like it."

"Forget it," June warned her. "Nobody's going nowhere until Penny and Ray get back. Which brings me to the high point of the evening," she said, brandishing the letter. "A communiqué from our revolutionary sister down on the coffee bean farm. Here," she tossed it to me, "you do the honors."

I opened it and read aloud:

"Dear Pam, June and Carole,

"I don't think I've ever worked so hard in my life. We get up at four a.m., before it's light, eat some rice and beans and start walking into the mountains to pick. Sometimes planes fly overhead—American military mostly. We're not far from the Honduran border and you really feel the contra presence. Earlier this week a man from the village where we're staying was ambushed and killed; two weeks ago almost a whole village, mainly women and kids, was wiped out. A lot of people carry guns here—they have to. They stand on duty while we pick. We pick all day until about four o'clock, thousands of bright red beans. I know I'm never going to drink a cup of coffee in the same way again.

"In the evenings we study Spanish and sometimes listen to talks on life before and after the revolution. I'm embarrassed by some of the Americans with us. They're not used to such hard work (neither am I, obviously), and complain all the time. One guy is in training to be a photo-journalist, I think. He goes around with three cameras around his neck, trying to pose everyone.

"The people are incredibly kind and patient with us. They keep saying, 'Can't you tell your government that we don't want to fight with them, we just want to live our lives in peace? It was enough that we had to make the revolution. Now let us just live it.' Something like seventy percent of their entire economy is going for defense right now. So many of the hopeful social programs of the last five years have had to be abandoned—all because of this stupid military threat from the U.S. The Nicaraguans consider us at war with them right now, though there are no American soldiers. Because of the economic boycott and because they're constantly living with the fear of invasion. But it is a war – about 6,000 people were killed last year alone.

"Ray and I are fine, though I've been sick a lot. At first I thought it was due to the high altitude or change in diet, but now it turns out I'm pregnant! ['Pregnant!' I stumbled, then continued.] I guess I'm going to keep it. I'd have to leave if I were going to have an abortion. And I don't want one anyway. I hope you'll all be happy for me. Pam, you'll be an aunt! Must go now. Lots of love, Penny."

"Our Penny, a mother!" June marveled. "Well, well, someone to carry on the family business. What's the matter, Pam, you don't look too cheerful."

"It's not that." I didn't know what I felt, actually. Glad for Penny, shocked, curious. I'd known it was bound to happen sometime. I just wasn't prepared. I looked at the two women sitting across from me at the table – happily coupled in their different ways – and thought, Well, at least Hadley's coming back.

Carole left early to meet Devlin (They were going to a travelogue on Indonesia), but June stayed to help wash the dishes, and I told her about Portland.

"The main thing is," I said, "is that I feel like I failed to get Trish to trust me. But I tried to be as nonjudgemental as possible. I've thought and thought about prostitution and I don't feel put off, the way I once did. I don't think badly of her – for anything she's done or that's been done to her."

"Maybe it's more a question of her thinking badly of herself. You know how, when you've sunk down low in your own estimation, ain't nobody can pull you back up. You're suspicious when somebody is nice to you, you think they must be putting you on if they say you're all right. Because inside you know you're a piece of shit."

"I've never felt that, anyway not so much that I couldn't fight back against those feelings."

"You're lucky then, if you don't get affected by a look on the street or somebody's mean words – and feel inside somehow that you deserve it."

"You? June, I can't believe it. You're the strongest person I know."

"I'm also a Black person." She paused and scrubbed hard at a pot, bending her sculpted dark head and neck over the sink. "But think about it — aren't there times, when you're reading a history book or looking at the newspapers and there's some mention of how women can't, women never — and in spite of knowing that that's all wrong, you think to yourself, Women can't, women never?"

"When you put it like that — who hasn't?"

"I don't go along with those who say things like all women are prostitutes," June continued, "cause we get married to support ourselves or have to trade sex for favors. But I believe you have to think about it sometimes from that angle. Ain't *no* woman alive who's living her life the way she wants to, the way she *could* be living it. If you think about it that way, you won't have to use words like 'nonjudgemental.' Because, when it comes down to it, you be in the same boat, honey. And we've all got to sink or swim together — never mind the mixed metaphor." June drained the water out. "So you don't have any idea where whoever it is could be hiding her?"

"The only thing I haven't tried today is calling her mother."

"Why don't you? I'll hang around."

Melanie was home alone and answered on the first ring. She was disappointed to hear it was me. "I've been waiting for Rob to call for hours. He didn't come home to dinner. I don't know where he can be."

"Is that like him?"

"No," she said immediately, then her worry got the better of her. "Well, he has been acting strange lately. I don't know what's come over him the past week. He says he's looking for work and then he doesn't come home. He doesn't want to talk to me about it, that's the worst part. I don't blame him really. It's not easy to find a job these days."

"Melanie. . ." I paused. What I was going to ask her was hard. "There was never anything between Rob and Trish, was there? From Rob's side. He didn't. . ."

"No!" She was outraged. "How could you think anything like that? I would have *known*. I mean, I told him about Art — he knew how much that would have upset me."

"Is that one reason you let Trish go out of your life so easily and stopped seeing her? Because you were afraid it would happen again? Because Rob convinced you she was a whore and nothing but a whore, and he couldn't be responsible for what happened?"

"I didn't let her go easily. It *wasn't* easy. I don't know how you can say such things. You're not a mother, or you'd know. It's never easy."

"Then help me," I said. "Help me find her. Is there any place at all you think she could be? That somebody could have taken her?"

Her anger was spent and she was crying. But finally she said, "I don't know. But if she's with Wayne...we have a cabin up above Index, in the Cascades. Wayne used to go up there until Rob made him give back the key..."

"Where exactly is it?"

She was reluctant to give me directions. "I don't know if Rob would like it. You going there."

"It may be a question of saving your daughter's life. At this point I don't know what somebody might do to her."

"But Rob..."

"Stop thinking of Rob for a minute and think of Trish. Please, Melanie."

She gave in and told me where the cabin was, probably not so much because she really believed that Trish was there, or that Trish was in danger, but because she was used to yielding. Or perhaps that was wrong. Maybe she really did think Rob had done something to her daughter and was just too afraid to say it.

38

INDEX WAS IN THE MOUNTAINS, a tiny town on the Skykomish River. It took us over an hour to get there, in spite of June's speed. There was snow and ice on the road; the night seemed very black. Index had a population of 169, according to its sign, a few stores and city buildings, a gas station and a tavern. Only the tavern was open.

"Go up the winding road on your left out of town," Melanie had said. "It's about two miles, but you may not be able to get through if there's a lot of snow."

She was right. Halfway out of town the road became undrivable. June wanted to turn back. "If we can't get through, neither could anybody else, especially not dragging Trish along."

"They could have walked. She might have gone willingly and he didn't have to drag her. They might have had snowshoes."

"They could have, but we don't. I say we go back to Index and call the Washington State Patrol."

"Not yet," I said. "We'll look stupid if she's not there."

"We'll look stupid if she *is* there and if the guy has a gun or something. In fact, we may look dead."

"Well, you can go back, but I'm going on. At least to see if there's a light in the window or anything." I got out of the car.

"You are too damned stubborn for your own good," she called after me. "Besides, you know I'd never let you go up there alone."

"Thanks, June."

"Sink or swim...I think I'm sinking," she added as she got out of the car and fell into a drift.

I helped her out and we started up the road.

The night was full of stars and frost; the black firs on either side wore coats of white and peaked white caps. As we stumbled up the slope I thought I saw footprints on the road, but we didn't have a flashlight and it was too dark to be certain.

"I don't know whether I want anybody to be there or not," June said. "What I'd really like is for a nice grandmotherly creature to fling open the door just as we get there and say, 'Pam and June! Just in time for a nice hot buttered rum!' "

"How's your training in outdoor survival?" I asked. "Do you know how to dig a snow cave for protection and conserve your body heat?"

"My people came from *Africa*, girl. We don't have those anti-cold genes like you reindeer hunters."

"Once, when Penny and I were twelve, our parents took us to Norway in the spring to visit relatives. That's the big skiing season, but that's also when they have all the avalanches. And every night on television they'd have these public service clips— showing families making snow caves and telling you how to survive until help came."

"I'm glad that at least one of us is prepared."

"Well, I never actually found myself in an avalanche...I think you're supposed to be carrying a lot of basic necessities. Food and extra clothes and stuff."

We chattered to keep from freezing and kept walking.

"Look," June said. "There's a cabin. You think that's it?"

A small one-room cabin with a shed full of wood attached huddled under a tall stand of firs. Through the window the flicker of a kerosene lamp was visible.

We crept silently up and looked inside, afraid to even whisper to each other.

The room was clean and cozy, with a couch, a big pine table and chairs, a bookshelf and a small wood stove. There was a

186

braided rug on the floor and a couple of pictures on the wall. No one was there.

June and I looked at each other and then she opened the door and we went in.

It was freezing cold and our heavy boots made the floor creak.

"Hello," I said, in too loud a voice. "Anybody here?"

"Somebody must have been here," said June, sounding relieved. "They must have just forgot the lamp."

"Wait," I said. I had noticed a loft with a ladder leading up to it. "Anybody up there?"

Silence. Neither June nor I could get up enough nerve to climb the ladder. But all of a sudden I became aware that someone was in the room was us, even though I couldn't hear breathing.

"Trish," I called cautiously. "Trish, are you up there? "

Nothing.

June picked up the ski pole that was standing by the door and pointed the sharp end of it towards the loft. Even in her heavy down jacket and beret there was something warrior-like about her. "I'm coming up," she said threateningly. She advanced up the ladder with the ski pole before her. Halfway up I heard her gasp.

"Oh, my god. Child, what has he done to you?"

She went all the way up and I followed at her heels.

Trish lay naked and gagged on a bare mattress. Her skin, even in the intermittant light of the kerosene lamp, was blueish and splotched with waxy white. Her eyes were half-closed and she was hardly breathing.

"Is she alive?"

"Barely, she's half froze to death. Quick, take off your jacket and go down and look for blankets or something." June lay next to Trish and held her. "You're gonna be all right, honey."

I found a sleeping bag downstairs and we wrapped her in it, then I went back down and fumbled with the wood stove, trying to start a fire. Who had left her here to freeze to death? Had she told him that she saw him kill Rosalie? Why hadn't he killed her right away then? Why this way, this cruel way? But maybe he wanted it to look like an accident. If he came back later and took the gag off and dressed her, no one would ever know. Probably he'd drugged her. People would just think that a poor teenage prostitute with a messed-up past and no future had taken too many downers, maybe on purpose, and had let the fire go out.

June came down the ladder. "She needs a doctor, but we can't take her outside in this cold. I'm going to get help. You find some tea or soup or anything hot and start feeding it to her. Keep the fire going and don't rub her, whatever you do. Friction's not good for frostbite."

June went out the door and was gone in the night. It would take her almost an hour to get to Index and probably another twenty minutes to get back if the State Patrol had a snowmobile or land rover. I pulled the couch in front of the door and went up the ladder.

Trish seemed to be responding slightly. Her eyes were still half-closed but her lips moved and she mumbled something.

"Trish, it's me. It's Pam. You're going to be all right. June's gone for help. She'll be back soon." She had started shaking convulsively and I hugged my body to hers, trying to warm her. After a few minutes the shakes subsided and she seemed to fall into a doze. I went downstairs and found a little jar of bouillon cubes, boiled water and made a cup of it.

"Trish, come on, wake up, drink this. It will make you feel better."

Her lips parted, but she couldn't help choking. I managed to get some of it down her. How long had June been gone? A half hour at least. Maybe it wouldn't take as long as I imagined. Ten minutes to town after she reached her car; and if it didn't take the State Patrol too long. . .

"Trish, it's Pam. Do you hear me?"

She succeeded in opening her eyes slightly, and I saw she recognized me.

"Pam," she croaked, and there was a kind of horror in her expression that I'd only seen in photographs of torture victims and concentration camp survivors. As if their humanness had been stripped away.

"I know, I know, but I'm here, it's all right. Just drink a little more of this. Don't try to talk now."

But she couldn't drink anymore and after a few seconds her eyes closed again and she seemed to fall asleep. I went down the ladder again, and then stopped.

I hadn't heard anyone come up to the cabin, but someone was turning the door knob. A man's voice, muffled, said, "Anybody here?"

I didn't answer, couldn't figure out whose voice it was.

The door knob rattled, harder now. "Karl, are you there? This is Wayne. I'm looking for Trish. For christssakes, is she all right?"

It had been Karl then. But where was he? Outside somewhere, on his way back? I didn't want to trust Wayne but I was more afraid of Karl than Wayne. I was especially afraid that June had met Karl on the road and that he'd done something to her. I might need Wayne's help.

"Wayne," I said. "This is Pam Nilsen. Are you alone?"

"Of course I'm alone," he said and his voice sounded young and anguished. "Please let me in—I've got to see if Trish is safe."

I pushed back the couch and opened the door.

39

Wᴀʏɴᴇ's ʜᴀɴᴅsᴏᴍᴇ ꜰᴀᴄᴇ was pale under his tan and his eyes were burning blue.

"I'm going to kill him," he said. "I couldn't believe it when he said Trish had called him and he'd gone down to Portland to get her. Why didn't she call *me*?"

"Calm down," I said. "You'll wake her."

His eyes darted anxiously to the loft. "Is that where she is? Are you sure she's all right?"

"She's fine—now," I said. "It looks like Karl just left her here to freeze to death. I don't know where he is. I hope he's not lurking around outside somewhere."

"Oh my god." Wayne sank down on a chair and buried his face in his hands. "If you knew what I'd been through tonight."

"How did you find out Karl had brought her here?"

"It occurred to me eventually. I'd given Karl the key to the place once and he must have made a copy. He didn't tell me when he called around seven. He was taunting me. Said he had Trish and wasn't going to tell me where. Said he was going to kill her. I was terrified. I'd taken Trish down to Portland to get her away from him. I knew he'd do the same thing to her as he'd done to Rosalie."

"So Karl killed Rosalie then?" Somehow it was all fitting together. "Only he didn't know it was Rosalie, he only knew her as Abby. Had she ripped him off somehow, muscled into his drug dealing?"

Wayne nodded, head still in his hands. He looked young and very vulnerable. "It's such a fucking long story," he said. "I don't even know where to begin."

"Start a year and a half ago, when you met him."

"I didn't know anything about him then," Wayne said in a low voice. "He was an artist from New York. I was impressed. But he had this big thing about how artists couldn't make any money through art. It was impossible. So he was going to deal coke, like he had in New York. He needed money to get started though. That's where Trish and I came in."

"So he was pimping both of you?"

"I'm not gay," Wayne murmured. "Not really. But it didn't seem so bad at first. We needed money. I never told Trish what I was doing. But after a while it seemed like it was really girls who could make more money. I was getting too old anyway. And Trish didn't seem to mind."

"Because she was hooked on you. She wanted to break away but she couldn't."

"That's not true! We really cared about each other!" Wayne raised his head. "You've got to believe that. I would never do anything to hurt her. I've always tried to help her. Karl would have run her into the ground. I tried to protect her as much as I could."

"So you recruited other girls to help. Was that how Rosalie came into the picture?"

Wayne nodded. "But she had other ideas. She didn't want to hook. She wanted in on the drug action. Finally Karl agreed. He set her up with some cash. She was supposed to give him fifty percent of the sale. The first few times it went okay. Then he found out she was holding back on him. He didn't tell me what he was going to do, but he arranged to meet Rosalie at that apartment building near the airport. What he didn't know was that Rosalie had asked Trish to come too, for protection. But somehow Trish didn't get there in time and . . . you know the rest."

"But Trish didn't actually see him."

"No. It was just me who figured out it was Karl. I didn't dare ask him if he'd seen Trish. I just wanted to get her out of Seattle. So when she called and said she was at your place I went and got her."

"And you never told her you thought Karl had killed Rosalie."

"No. I didn't want to scare her."

"Why didn't you tell the police?"

"And have my whole connection to Karl dragged out? My dad could maybe understand about the drugs, but not that Karl was gay, not me going with men for money. I couldn't take him knowing that!"

Wayne bent his head almost to his knees and rocked back and forth, making a low, anguished sound.

I couldn't help it, I felt sorry for him. In spite of everything he'd done to Trish, in spite of his screwing me around for days. I went over to him and put my hand on his shoulder.

"It's all right," I said. "It's going to be all right."

There was a silence broken only by his strangled moans, then, from the loft above, came the small cracked whisper, "He's lying."

Afterwards, like all victims, I went over and over the events, looking for things I should or shouldn't have done. I *shouldn't* have opened the door, not to anyone except June. I *shouldn't* have believed anything he said. I *should* have fought back harder. I *shouldn't* have let it happen to me. I was stupid, I could have gotten away if I'd really tried. I was weak and cowardly and a woman. I deserved it.

He picked up the ski pole and said, "I'll stab you if you struggle." He lunged for me and pinned me down on the floor, tied my hands with rope from his pocket and gagged me with a kitchen towel.

I couldn't believe it was happening. Even though I knew now what he had done to Trish and Rosalie, a part of me kept seeing the tanned, smiling young artist in the Hawaiian shirt, the vulnerable little boy. He wasn't smiling now, he wasn't crying either; his eyes were dry and the once caressing playboy gaze was cold and hard and full of hatred.

"You never fooled me," he said. "Not with your *Jane Eyre* or your coke deal. You never bought coke in your life. You were just spying on me. And I hate spies."

He slapped my face and brought tears to my eyes.

"I should have known you'd come following Trish up here. You fucking dyke. She told me about you. Told me you'd tried to get her to stay with you. And then you followed her down to Portland and got the cops involved. She wasn't going to say anything about Rosalie until you put the idea in her head. Now I can't trust her."

He slapped me again, so hard my head jerked back. All I could think was, June, please come soon, please.

"Yeah, I killed Rosalie. You want to know why? The bitch wanted Trish off the streets; she said she and Trish should get a piece of the action. Like Trish belonged to her or something, the fucking nigger whore. Trish belongs to *me*." Wayne's lips tightened to a streak of white and he picked up the ski pole and swung it towards me, missing my forehead by about an inch. "That's what she thought. I found out where she was holing up in somebody's apartment on the strip. I didn't know she and Trish were supposed to be meeting that night. I got out the side window but not before I saw Trish. I didn't think she'd seen me, but I knew, even if she had, she wouldn't tell." He swung the ski pole in my face again and I closed my eyes. "It was you who put that idea into her head, so I couldn't trust her. And now you're going to end up just like Rosalie. A lesson to Trish. You hear that bitch?" he called up the ladder. "If you ever try to get away from me again you'll be next."

Wayne was almost starting to enjoy himself now. He put down the ski pole, took off his down jacket and removed a syringe and a tourniquet and a baggie of coke from his pocket. He mixed the coke with water in a spoon and heated it over the wood stove. Then he tied off his arm and shot himself up. And all the while he was talking.

"I can't believe you suspected Karl. Karl couldn't do shit. He's just a drunk. The only thing I was afraid of was he'd tell you I was in Portland. Yeah, I took her there, and I picked her up too, when she called me. She didn't know who else to call. She can't do anything without me. Can you, bitch?" he shouted up at the loft.

Then he turned to me. "I've thought about this for a long time," he said. "When you came with that game of buying the coke. If you hadn't had your friend with you I would have. But this is going to be even better. By the time I get done with you you're going to be sorry you were ever born."

He raped me. With a punishing violence that had nothing to do with sex and everything to do with rage and hatred. My vagina was as dry as my mouth and every pounding blow stabbed through my body like a sword dipped in fire. It was like surgery without anesthesia, like nothing I'd ever felt. I almost blanked out; my whole being reduced to a tiny pinprick that cried out *no.*

"Bitch, cunt, lezzie, pervert, whore, how do you like this, you fucking dyke." The cocaine and his fury made him demonic; he slapped my face over and over and thrust into me again- and again. It seemed endless; a world of pain spread through my back, down my legs. I felt that whatever made Pam a person, whatever I knew or had known about myself was being crushed out of me, was spinning into fragments like a planet smashed by meteors.

Then June burst through the door; she picked up the ski pole and struck at him, on the back, on the arms. If the State Patrol officers, right behind her, hadn't stopped her, she would have killed him. I'm sure of that.

40

RAPE IS SOMETHING YOU RECOVER FROM, but at first you don't believe you ever will. It haunts you like a nightmare that has no waking end. Over and over I saw myself as the patrolmen must have seen me, pants down, bleeding and exposed. Degraded and exposed. One of them, I'm positive, was turned on. I saw it in his eyes. And strangely enough, it's his expression I remember most. I can't really remember the hatred on Wayne's face and the ripping feeling I had inside. It's buried too deep. But I remember the secret glint in the officer's eyes; I can't seem to forget it.

If it had been *Cagney and Lacey*, the show would have stopped right there, with the dramatic moment of rescue. But somehow it didn't. I had to go on living. And living was hard.

I had back pains and pains that shot down my legs. The entrance to my vagina was torn and my face was battered black and blue. I was afraid of noises and of the dark and I couldn't stand to look at men; even passing them in the street scared me. I knew they weren't all rapists, but it didn't matter. Right after you've been raped you don't feel quite the same about men; you don't feel quite the same about your body either, you don't feel that it's totally yours. Some boundary has been violated; a boundary you used to feel was strong and indestructible feels more like tissue paper, easily torn.

I didn't feel "good" anymore. I felt "bad." In other people's eyes anyway; in the eyes of the patrolmen, in the eyes of the doctor and nurses at the emergency room, even in the eyes of some of my friends. They were there to help me; they felt pity and they tried to be supportive, but I still felt I was the one who'd transgressed, that I was one who'd done something unspeakably wrong. Being a victim doesn't make you self-righteous; it makes you defensive, suspicious, ashamed. I felt like people knew something about me that I didn't want known, like they could use it against me. I felt I would never be just Pam again. I would be "Pam who was raped, did you hear about it?"

Of course I was saved, I wasn't killed; I wasn't pregnant either, I was grateful for that. We were all saved, Trish, me, June. Not Rosalie though. And Wayne was in jail, with counts of murder, rape and attempted murder against him. If we were lucky he'd be behind bars for years after the trial.

But it didn't make me feel better, at least in the weeks right after the rape, knowing that I'd found Rosalie's murderer, that I'd found Trish. I would have preferred it to have been Rob or Karl who was an evil, woman-hating killer. I would have preferred it to have been anyone but Wayne, who I'd believed and tried to comfort.

Because that made it worse.

Carole tried to help. She took me to her self-defense class and wanted to practice karate moves with me at the shop. But my body hurt too much. When I saw her coming towards me with her arm upraised my heart stopped and I wanted to scream. I couldn't defend myself.

"Hit me, Pam," she urged. "You're angry. You want to kill. Let it out."

But I couldn't hit her. I could only shrink back. The anger was deep inside, paralyzing me. I wanted to kill. I wanted to kill Wayne very badly. But I wasn't going to be able to.

*

It was Beth who helped me first, Beth and Janis, who'd decided she was moving to Seattle. They took me to the ocean one weekend in late January. While Janis ran up and down the beach with her delighted terrier, Beth and I walked slowly in the wet sand. She held my hand, and she talked about herself. I could tell it was hard for her.

"I was raped too. A long time ago, when I was eighteen, after I'd moved to San Francisco. It wasn't as violent as what happened to you, but it was pretty bad. I couldn't have sex for a couple of years after that. The worst thing was that it was the man who I was so crazy in love with who did it."

"How did you deal with it?"

"I didn't. I didn't tell anyone. I tried to push it out of my mind. By not having sex I didn't have to think about it. It was only twelve or thirteen years later that I even remembered it had happened. You're only the second person I've ever told." She watched Janis throw a stick to the dog. "She's the first."

"Do you think—that Wayne raped Trish too?"

"I don't know. Why don't you ask her?"

"But it's so personal."

"So is what happened to you."

I didn't say anything. It felt good to be on the foggy beach. The white breakers came in with a violent crash and slipped away again like ice melting. The sun came out at intervals, like a pebble someone kept tossing up into the sky.

I had only seen Trish twice in the two weeks since the incident at the cabin. At the hearing where we'd both testified against Wayne she'd kept her head lowered as she'd told the story. It was very simple really. Rosalie had tried to help Trish get out of prostitution and Wayne had killed her because of that. She hadn't wanted to believe it, but she believed it now.

She was living at the runaway shelter on Beacon Hill and receiving extensive counseling. I called and asked her if she'd like to get together for dinner.

"Ernesto misses you." I paused. "And so do I."

She came and met me at the shop at five, wearing her familiar black hat and jeans. Her triangular face was almost bare of makeup.

"Hi, Trish," said June, unusually gentle. Ever since that night she'd been walking around on eggshells, treating me like an invalid. I didn't want her pity but found it difficult to talk with her about what had happened. Maybe I was upset to think she'd seen me being raped. Maybe I couldn't help blaming her somehow for not getting there ten minutes earlier.

"Hi," said Trish shyly. Did she remember how June had held her and talked to her?

We drove up to Capitol Hill without talking much. She said she liked the shelter, that she'd given up smoking. "Cigarettes make me sick!"

I wondered if she'd changed her mind about green vegetables. To be on the safe side I'd prepared cream cheese enchiladas that just needed to be heated up.

"It seems like years since I was here," she said, coming into the living room. But Ernesto hadn't forgotten her. He bounded over and threw himself at her feet like a raccoon cap, purring wildly.

"Hi boy, hi, hi." She bent and stroked him.

"I heard from my sister in Nicaragua," I said suddenly. "She's having a baby. It's going to be strange to be an aunt."

"It's going to be strange to be a sister," she said. "My mom's due in about a month. You know, she came and visited me... We talked..."

We were both polite, hesitant, afraid of treading new ground. I felt an awkwardness I hadn't had when I was trying to save her from herself. A new vulnerability.

"That woman I mentioned, Hadley. She's coming back to Seattle in February..."

"That's great," said Trish. "...Did you tell her—about what happened?"

I shook my head. "No, not yet. It's kind of hard to talk about."

"I know."

"Listen, Trish, I found your diary in Rosalie's room and your dad gave me the one you left behind. I read them." I pulled the little books out of the shelf and gave them to her. "I'm sorry. I was trying to find you—and they did help."

She took them without apparent emotion. "Sometimes I told the truth in them. There were a lot of things I never wrote. I've started a new one now. I'm going to try to be honest."

"When I was your age..." I didn't like the sound of that and began again. "I used to keep a diary but I stopped a long time ago. I've been thinking of starting one. There are a lot of things I can't seem to talk about. I thought that if I wrote them..."

"About Wayne?"

I nodded.

"You know, it's weird," she said, stroking Ernesto and not quite looking at me. "When I was up in the loft, when he was—doing it to you—I felt like it was happening to me, more than when it did happen to me. I mean, it hurt me that it was Wayne who did it to me, but it had happened to me so many times that I was used to it. A long time ago I stopped feeling anything. I just went away in my head. Having sex didn't feel like it had anything to do with me. But when I heard you struggling and moaning and heard what Wayne was saying to you, it was like I felt it was happening to me. And it hurt me in a new way. Like it was the first time I really felt it."

I had started crying, helplessly, as the memory of that night went through me again. Trish came over and stood next to me, clumsily holding my arm and then putting her arm around my shoulders. She was taller than me and smelled very young.

"Come on, come on," she said. "You're still *you*, no matter what happened. And nobody can take that away from you." She began to cry too, "For a long time I didn't know that. I let everybody tell me, I let Wayne tell me, You're no good, you're a whore, you're stupid, you're never going to get off drugs. I thought it was my own voice telling me those things, but it wasn't. It was his, it was theirs. And I don't have to listen to it anymore."

It had been so long since I'd had anybody to hold me, so long since I had been able to admit that I needed any kind of help at all. I stopped thinking that *I* was the one who was older, that I was supposed to be protecting her. I held her. I let her hold me, and cried myself out.

Afterwards we had dinner and she ate all her salad. Later we made popcorn and played a game of Scrabble. Ernesto sat in Trish's lap; he purred like he could never get enough.

41

THE NEXT DAY AT WORK I TOLD JUNE, "Okay, I'm through acting like a crushed grape and you don't have to treat me like that anymore either. Let's talk about what you felt."

"Guilty," she said. "That I'd left you alone, that I hadn't gotten back sooner. I could have killed that motherfucker. I would have killed him, too, if the cops hadn't been there."

"Do you think it could have happened to you?" I expected her to say no. She was, after all, stronger than me, tougher; she would have grabbed the ski pole away from him and stabbed him in the eye before he could have tied her up.

"Yes," she said. "I do. It keeps going through my head over and over, 'It could have been me, I'm so glad it wasn't me . . .' I used to think rape was something that happened to stupid people. But you're not stupid, no more stupid than me anyway. We never should have gone up there alone."

"Trish would have been dead then."

"I know. I know."

We were silent, each of us struggling to come to some acceptance of what had happened, looking for a way to move forward.

"Are you going skydiving this weekend?" I suddenly asked.

"If the weather's good...Why? You want to come along?"

"Yeah, I do." I couldn't believe I was saying this. "I'm thinking about jumping."

My body felt frozen, broken, useless. I needed to do something that would wake it up again and release it.

It wasn't as easy—or as hard—as simply strapping on a parachute and leaping. I had to go through a long training session with certified instructors in a classroom situation.

They showed slides and made diagrams. They hooked me and the other students into parachutes and made us hang from the ceiling. The straps between my legs cut into my newly removed stitches and hurt like hell. Then we spent two hours learning to jump, first from a height of four feet, then from six feet. Over and over the instructor drilled us, "Land with your feet together, crouch and roll to the side." Then we got into a little pretend airplane and practiced some more.

They were leaving very little up to chance. No telling what you'd remember once you got up in the air. We had parachutes on our backs that opened automatically and parachutes on our chests that we could pull with an emergency tab. We even had small radios strapped to us, so they could guide us through the jump and tell us where to land. We were supposed to aim for a gravel pit that had arrows around it. We were not supposed to land in the motel swimming pool, the trees or, god forbid, the freeway.

June went up with me. The airplane seemed even smaller and more fragile than before, angling up sharply, incredibly noisy. My stomach felt like a deflated, quivering balloon and every nerve resisted what I was about to do.

I thought about Penny coming home in a week and how glad I'd be to see her, about being an aunt, about Hadley and what might happen between us. I thought about what I'd learned from Trish, and from Beth and Janis. I even thought about Carole and how in a funny way we were friends, after all. Anything to stop from thinking about how high up we were and how there was nothing, absolutely nothing, to hold me between heaven and earth.

"Ready, Pam? You're first." June squeezed my arm and her brown eyes were full of excitement and compassion. "I love you, babe. I'm proud of you. See you on the ground."

I hung on to the wing strut a moment and then let go. I fell straight down, leaving my heart somewhere above me, fluttering out like the tiny lead parachute.

One thousand one, one thousand two, one thousand three, one thousand four, one thousand. . . The main parachute opened with a soft jerk and suddenly everything was very quiet and I could see. I was caught, floating, safe. Safe, like Penny had said.

I was flying, free and easy, and the earth looked very beautiful from here.